Liza and Libby:

The Adventures Begin

Alexandra M. Wallace

Illustrations by Elizabeth Maxim

Liza and Libby: The Adventures Begin
Text copyright © 2022 by Alexandra M. Wallace
Illustrations copyright © 2022 by Elizabeth Maxim
Photo copyrights @ 2022 by Alexandra M. Wallace

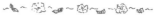

Elizabeth Maxim has been drawing horses, flowers and mountains and sharing her artistic gift with friends and family since forever. Her favorite medium is pen and ink and watercolor, and her work captures the magic of the stories and settings of the authors with whom she works.

Published by Pondera Publishing, LLC

For information regarding permission write to:
Pondera Publishing, LLC
Attention: Permissions Department
P.O. Box 204, Penns Creek, PA 17862

Hardcover: ISBN: 979-8-9855986-0-5
Paperback: ISBN: 979-8-9855986-1-2
Audiobook: ISBN: 979-8-9855986-2-9

Library of Congress Control Number: 2022930900

To write to Liza or Libby:
www.LizaandLibby.com
(They would love to hear from you.)

Printed in the USA

www.PonderaPublishing.com

This is the page of many important things.
Now go off and enjoy the adventures contained within.
Liza and Libby hope you have a wonderful time reading!

To the one true horse who taught me love,
compassion, resilience and tenderness.

CHAPTER ONE

OUT WEST

She turned her head and saw a nose. It was that lovely, soft, wonderful nose she knew so well. Liza loved that nose.

The nose was white and fuzzy, and was nuzzling gently, ever so gently, and it was leaning forward to touch Liza's cheek as if to say, "Hello my friend!" The breathing was audible and very comforting. The whiskers gently brushed against Liza and Liza looked into the most beautiful soft brown eyes she had ever seen.

Liza was twelve years old. She was strong and smart. She had long flowing hair which was often blown about madly by the wind. Sometimes her hair was tousled under a cowboy hat and sometimes she just pinned it up quickly in a barrette or with an elastic tie. She walked with a long confident stride. She had purpose in her manner. She moved with the sleekness of a mountain lion and had the strength of one too. She was a happy young lady, a pre-teen, but a young lady nonetheless.

The incredible creature that was nuzzling her was a strong ten-year-old quarter horse named Libby. Libby was a beautiful sorrel with white markings on her face just like a paint horse. She was 14.3 hands high and her body was all muscle. And she was a mare like no other. She was never mean. She was sometimes bossy to the other horses, but only when they asked for it. With her excellent quarter horse bloodlines, she was physically strong and confident, just like Liza was.

Liza and Libby. They were a wonderful team and they were quite the partnership. And they had a strong bond of love that was everlasting.

It was a quiet morning in Arizona. Liza and her family were there for the wintertime. They had set up camp near a mountainous area and Liza was out taking care of the horses. She had on a light jacket due to the cool brisk morning air. She walked toward the corral with purpose because Liza had daily morning chores. She wore well-used and sensible cowboy boots. Her jeans were comfortable with some cowgirl decorations on them made of crystals. Liza called those decorations "bling". Every cowgirl wore bling of some kind or another. Liza was also wearing a warm long-sleeved shirt under a comfortable jacket that had many pockets.

She always had her cowboy hat on to keep off the sun and to offer some protection from the elements. Mostly, it kept the sun off her nose and it kept her warm on mornings like this. She never minded a cool morning. The days were warm but nights and mornings had a slight chill.

Liza's family traveled in a big, four-horse trailer with a long living quarters area. That meant the family had a living area inside like a proper RV - recreational vehicle - at the front of the trailer, and the horses all traveled in their own stalls at the back of the trailer. All of the saddles and bridles and other equine supplies were in a separate tack area at the back as well.

The living quarters had beds, a couch, a large kitchen, and a spacious bathroom with a big shower. Their trailer was fully functional like any RV with electricity, propane and running water. It was just like a traveling home on wheels. Even though it was roomy and comfortable, they packed wisely with just enough of everything but not too much of any one thing.

Liza was always amazed at how practical her family was. The family packed clothing for different seasons, and packed enough tack and supplies for all the horses. Though practical, there were hidden surprises stored in the trailer as well, such as the Easter basket her mother had prepared for her last year. Somewhere, tucked away in storage, her mother even had a little Christmas tree packed with some tiny pretty flashing lights.

Liza had her own bunk bed in the back of the living quarters area. She had books there piled in a corner of her bunk. Thanks to her own little reading light, she spent a lot of time reading, when she had spare time. A stuffed horse was her bedtime companion. Liza knew she was getting older but never gave it a moment's notice that she still had a favorite stuffed horse along with her on the road. "Why of course I have one," she sometimes thought. "Who wouldn't have one!" she would say.

In her little bunk area, Liza also had some pretty horsey lights hanging around her window. She could turn them on anytime she wanted. The horses were all different colors and they glowed and gave off a nice warm feeling at night. Sometimes she would lie there looking out the window, framed by her horsey lights, as she thought about her day.

Just behind the wall where she slept were the stalls for the horses. While the family drove, all the horses were there in the stalls. They stood and munched on hay and drank their own water while traveling.

On this trip, Liza and her family had traveled all across country to get to their winter destination in Arizona. They had spent four days and three nights on the road.

The family would stay overnight with friends who had ranches along their route, and the horses would be unloaded to stay in stalls each night of the trip.

Liza loved to travel. She was good at identifying landmarks and at reading maps. This was their third time across country to spend the winter in Arizona. She had already made plans in her head of the trail rides she wanted to do with her horse Libby.

Now, at their camping spot, the horses were outside in portable pens. Water buckets were hanging carefully for each horse. The horses were given plenty of hay because in the area where they were camping, there was no grass for forage within the portable pens. There were scrub trees and cacti all around and mountains in the near distance. Liza was certain she saw a coyote or two skulking about. She kept her eye out for them but didn't worry too much.

Inside the trailer, the family was getting up. Liza's parents slept in the front of the trailer up in what was called the gooseneck. This was the part of the trailer that was up and over the bed of the truck. Liza's non-horsey friends always found the word "gooseneck" to be a funny name. But it certainly made for a very nice master bedroom.

Liza was usually the first to arise. She had pulled on her jeans and boots and other clothing. She had quietly stepped into the bath area and washed her face, brushed her teeth, combed her hair and then hung her wash towel. Then Liza had gone outside for morning chores.

This young cowgirl loved every minute of her farm chores. Being on the road was one of her favorite things. To

Liza, being on the road meant heading off with her family, in truck and trailer, heading to distant locations with horses in the back. And it meant she could walk right outside her door and boom! The horses were right there in their pens next to the horse trailer! She loved that.

First, she cleaned and refilled the water buckets and made a mental note of how much each horse drank. She tossed hay into each pen and said a warm hello to each horse. Then, grabbing a pitchfork and a wheelbarrow, she picked each pen clean, also noting the manure situation. Was it formed into balls or was it runny?

When you were on the road with horses, as Liza called it, their health was very important and knowing how much water they drank and how their manure looked was often the first sign of whether the horse was getting sick or not. Everyone looked great today!

After she had done her morning chores, she headed back to the trailer.

"Good morning, Papa," she cried.

"Good morning, my little one," her father said. "Are the horses all doing well?" he asked.

"Yes sir," she said.

Her father was already up and dressed and was outside checking on the water and electrical connections to the trailer. He had his tire pressure gauge out and had walked around the trailer to check the tires. Although he knew the trailer was level, he checked it again in case he needed to add some levelers under the wheels to make it more comfortable. If the trailer wasn't level, Liza and her family could feel it as they slept at night!

Liza looked all around her. "I really am a very lucky cowgirl," she thought. "Look how I get to live! I study while I am on the road. I ride my horses almost every day." She felt blessed. And she looked up into the sky and said, "Thank you!"

Just at that moment, she could smell potatoes being cooked. She loved home fries! Her mother made the best home fries in the world, according to Liza. Her mother would boil the potatoes up the night before, then cube them into small pieces and then fry them over a cast iron frying pan the next morning. Liza enjoyed cooking and helping with meal preparation. And even though Liza helped her mother, Liza knew that she needed a lot of practice to come close to making tasty meals equal to what her mother cooked.

"Oh Mama!!!" Liza cried. "That smells delicious!"

The main door to the trailer was open and the screen door was shut but her mother could hear her.

"Thank you, my pumpkin," her mother said. She had peaked her head around the corner and Liza could see her mother through the screen door. Liza loved breakfasts. Best meal of the day she always thought.

Liza went over to the trailer and cleaned off her boots at the door, then opened the screen door and went inside, closing the door carefully behind her. Except for butterflies, dragonflies, praying mantises, katydids and honeybees, she did not like flying insects too much, especially flies and mosquitos. You never knew what might be up and out flying about even on a chilly morning in Arizona. She liked to keep the screen door closed.

Liza opened pantry doors and pulled out dishes and forks and knives and laid the table for her family. Her mother passed Liza some napkins and a cup of coffee for her father for Liza to place on the table. Liza grabbed some orange juice from the refrigerator for herself.

After a few moments, her father came back into the living quarters and joined them. He never added milk or sugar to his coffee. Liza's father liked his coffee black and strong. Just like the cowboys from long ago, he used to say. Their coffee was barefooted! Liza had already added some milk and a tiny bit of sugar to her mother's coffee and put it at her mother's place setting. Liza knew her mother liked coffee just a little bit light and a little bit sweet. But not too sweet and not too light.

At breakfast, the family discussed their plans for the day. This morning, Liza knew they were taking a trail ride and she was pretty excited about it. During breakfast, she pulled out their trail maps and showed them to her family.

"It looks like this one trail goes up into the hills and should give us a few hours of great trail riding," she said to her parents. "We can head right out of camp and get up into the lower hills over yonder pretty quickly," Liza added.

"That works for me," said her father. He rode a dun horse named Dude. "I'd like to see Dude get stretched out today," her father continued. "He's in good shape but I'd like to get him climbing a bit so those trails you have chosen there, Liza, well they look pretty good for Dude."

"I'm happy with those trails too," her mother said. Liza's mother had a paint horse named Belle. "Belle can out-climb both of you and we will put Dude and Libby to the test for sure," she said as she gave a wink to Liza. Her mother knew not to push the horses too soon and too fast after a long haul in the trailer.

In fact, today, everyone knew that as for today's ride, well, it was just to stretch their horse's legs and to get them breathing a bit and working their muscles.

"I'm thinking Libby and I need to walk a while at first, but then I'd like to get her long trotting if that's okay," Liza said to her parents. They both nodded.

"Good then," said her father. "After we clean up, let's pack some supplies and head out."

Liza helped clear the table and then her mother began doing the dishes while her father put the leftovers away.

Liza and her family had a full hook up where they were camping, which meant they had water, electric and sewer connections at their horse camping site. And although they had full access to water, after so many years of dry camping – using your own supplies and energy – they still conserved water even when washing dishes off of a direct water source.

As her parents finished up in the kitchen, Liza headed back to her bunk area and grabbed some extra clothing as well as her leather bag which she could clip onto the back of her saddle. She had designed the bag herself and was pretty pleased with it. It had a functional look to it but still had a sense of cowgirl style. She had asked the leather maker to add some fringe to it and it was all secured with snaps and hooks. It was durable but soft leather. Designed for use and with care, Liza knew it would last a long time.

In the kitchen, her parents were organizing some snacks and drinks for the trail ride which they would tuck into each of their saddlebags. They usually packed crackers, nuts, raisins, some hard cheese, and always had some chocolate with them too.

Her mother also had a trail riding first aid kit for them and a separate one for the horses. "Liza, would you please grab the equine first aid kit and secure it to your saddle horn for our trail ride this time?" her mother asked.

"I'll take the other kit," her father said.

"Sure, Mama," Liza said. She didn't mind. She had designed the leather bag for this kit and Liza knew it would connect easily to her pommel on her saddle.

"I'm ready," she said to her mother.

Food, water and equine first aid kit in hand, with some extra clothing as well, Liza headed out the door and her parents followed. Liza put the items she needed on top of the outside table and went to get her horse Libby ready to ride. Here at the campsite, the family used the tack room of their trailer to tack up the horses. Back home, they had a large tack area in their barn for storing their saddles, bridles, and other equine supplies.

But first, Liza walked to the back of the trailer and stepped up on the ramp and dialed the code of the lock on the tack area door. The back of the trailer had two large doors. The large one on the right gave access to the part of the trailer for the horses. The one on the left was to the tack room area where they stored saddles, pads, bridles and other horse supplies. She opened the tack door and as it swung open and wide, she secured it to the side of the trailer with a hook. Then she pulled out the curry brushes for the three horses and laid them on the edge of the ramp.

Her mother had been to the three horse paddocks and was bringing out Belle already as well as Libby. Her father was right behind with Dude.

"Hi ya girl," Liza said again when her mother handed Libby's lead rope to Liza. "Come on over here with me." Libby nickered when Liza took the rope.

Liza walked over to the large hitching post that was near the edge of the campsite and guided Libby to walk beside her. She looped the lead rope around the rail and secured Libby. Then using her hoof pick, she began to groom Libby. As Liza slid her hand down Libby's leg, Liza leaned gently into the side of Libby and Libby easily lifted her leg up to have her hoof picked.

"Easy girl," Liza said.

Liza made her way around Libby checking her legs to look for any scrapes or bruises. She bent down next to each leg and gently lifted each hoof to pick it, clean it and to look for bruising, tenderness or an abscess. Liza visually inspected each shoe to look for loose nails or to see if the shoe had shifted or see if it had been bent or ripped off accidentally. "Yours are nice and secure," Liza said to Libby. Libby turned her head to look back at Liza. Liza smiled at her mare. "We just had the farrier out for new shoes for you, girl, so you are all set," Liza said to Libby. Libby nickered again and closed her eyes.

Liza had a pretty good routine to really check her mare's hooves. What she did exactly was she slid her hand over Libby's back, across her rump and along her side. Then she would slide her hand down Libby's leg, lean into her a little bit, and Libby would lift her leg. Liza used a hoof pick and brush to clean out the hoof and around the shoe to gently remove any debris. With easy pressure and a soothing tone, Liza would go about her work to pick hooves. Keeping hooves strong and clean and without any bruises was important. Liza not only looked for any looseness in the shoes but carefully looked to see if any stones were caught underneath. Since all of their horses had just been freshly shod a few days before their big trip, Libby was good for another six weeks of riding or so before she needed a trim and reset.

Libby was an easy keeper. That meant she wasn't fussy. She ate her grain and slowly ate her hay and she actually kept her pen pretty clean, for a horse. She drank plenty of water even when she was being hauled on the trailer. And if she ever needed medicine, she took it like a champion.

As she thought about her horse, Liza pulled out her curry brush and started to curry along Libby's back and neck and belly and rump. Currying was her favorite part of grooming. Liza murmured some soothing words to Libby as she curried her horse. Liza's movements were methodical and practiced and predictable. She followed a pattern as she moved all around Libby's body. Liza scanned Libby from head to tail to hoof, looking for any bruises or signs of soreness or any scruffs or even signs of rain rot or other skin conditions.

Liza liked to tend to anything that looked out of place. Liza took great care of Libby. Liza's methodical and calm motions of her work soothed Libby. Liza could tell because Libby's eyes were closed.

"Silly girl, are you falling asleep again? Wake up sleepyhead," Liza teased. Libby would often close her eyes and sometimes fell asleep as Liza curried her. Liza always thought that was a funny thing.

As Liza curried Libby, every now and then Libby licked her lips. Liza knew that meant Libby was relaxed.

Sometimes Libby would turn her head slightly to look at Liza. Liza would stop and say hello again and step forward to pet Libby's forehead or nose. "You're such a good girl," Liza would say.

When she finished picking hooves and scanning Libby's body, and when she finished currying and checking to make sure the saddle area was free of debris, Liza felt that she was all set to start to tack up.

Liza walked back across the gravel over to the tack storage area of the trailer and grabbed her saddle pad and walked back and laid it on Libby. Then she returned to the trailer and grabbed her saddle and breast collar and walked over to Libby again and carefully swung it up and laid it across Libby's back.

Liza fussed with the location of the saddle pad and the saddle until it was in the exact perfect spot. Liza always looked at the contour of Libby's back and withers to be certain the pad and saddle would rest comfortably on her.

Liza secured the cinch and tucked the leather latigo into its place in the rigging. Liza never pulled it up too tightly. One time she did that and Libby actually winced. Liza always pulled it up and left it slightly loose at first, then waited and made one more tug. Securing the breast collar and back cinch, Liza was almost ready to go.

But first, she grabbed Libby's bell boots and both sets of protective splint boots and secured them into place.

Liza grabbed her leather packs from the table near the trailer and walked back over to Libby. First, she secured the pack across the back of the saddle just behind the cantle on the skirt. She wrapped two leather straps around it even as she hooked it into place. Then she flopped the saddlebag back over the pommel and secured it. One side held the equine first aid kit, while the other held some of the snacks that her parents had prepared for the trail ride. Her two water bottles fit in each side of the bag. "You can never have too much water," Liza thought.

Then Liza grabbed a heavier longer jacket from inside the trailer and also secured it to the back of her saddle. Her parents had already tacked up Dude and Belle and had secured their leather packs and spare jackets to their horses as well.

The last thing Liza did was to remove Libby's halter and put on Libby's bridle. She fixed Libby's forelock so it wasn't all squished under the leather straps and also made sure the bit was seated properly in Libby's mouth. She put the leather reins up and over on one side and then the other and crossed them on the saddle. She fixed a concho that wasn't tight and secure.

Then she folded up the halter and lead rope and tied it all together with a leather strap hanging from a D-ring at the back of the saddle. It was snug and out of the way.

Liza checked the cinch again and snugged it one more hole then reached up and put her foot into the stirrup and expertly stepped up and swung her other leg over Libby's back. "Whoa girl," Liza said. "No need to walk on."

Liza already had the reins in her hand and with careful soft pressure on the reins, she asked Libby to tuck her nose. Then Liza asked Libby to step back a little bit then said, "Whoa." Libby responded nicely. "You're a good girl," Liza said and patted Libby on the side of her neck. Liza paused for a moment and slid her hand under Libby's mane. Liza leaned forward and continued to slide her hand up and under the mane. It felt all warm in there.

Libby was always so nice and warm. That made Liza feel safe and secure. It was hard to explain but Liza always felt so good when she ran her hands over Libby. Libby nickered a little bit and although she stood still, Liza could feel that Libby was ready to go.

"A few days of travel and you want to ride on out, don't ya girl?" said Liza. Liza squiggled her butt around in the saddle and got herself all comfortable and made sure her feet were properly in the stirrups, remembering to keep her heels down and to sit up with excellent posture.

"Ready Mama? Ready Papa?" Liza asked.

"You bet, Liza!" her parents said, practically in unison.

And with that, Liza let Libby walk on.

CHAPTER TWO

THE TRAIL RIDE BEGINS

Following a small trail, Liza went on up ahead of her parents and looked out into the countryside. It was beautiful there. Liza loved the peace and quiet and lovely beauty of each of the places where her parents camped over the years. They had traveled to different parts of the United States and Liza was already enjoying her trip out here to Arizona once again. The air was dry and slightly dusty.

This time of year, the flowers were beginning to bloom. Cactus flowers were everywhere. White ones and yellow ones in all shapes and sizes were in full bloom. Liza saw some on the side of the trail just now as she and Libby walked away from camp. Depending on which part of the trail she rode on, at different times of the year there were also colorful flowers closer to the ground. Of course, that depended on the rain. Either way, it made everything look so pretty against a harshly stark landscape.

Liza slid her hand down to her jacket zipper and gave it a little tug upwards. It was still a little chilly. She was glad for her jacket. Just before she left, Liza had actually grabbed two jackets. Her light jacket, which was on right now, and a heavier one, which she had just tied to the leather pack behind the cantle. Liza kind of smiled to herself. "Why did I pack a second jacket?" she wondered. She laughed. It didn't matter. Better to have a little more than a little less sometimes!

Liza felt the slight breeze and turned to look back at her parents. Dude and Belle were keeping up with Libby's pace though her parents had gotten on their horses a little after Liza had. Liza could see her parents but they were perhaps twenty or more yards behind her.

"I don't think Mama and Papa will mind if we pick up a trot, my girl, do you?" Liza asked Libby.

"I heard that," said her father. "Wait for us, Liza."

"I will, Papa," she said.

But Liza whispered to Libby, "Let's go. They will keep up."

With a gentle squeeze of her legs, Liza brought Libby up into a light jog and Liza collected Libby a little bit and then Liza began to post. Liza was working on Libby's top line so she had her slightly collected.

"This is good for you, Libby my girl. It helps make you stronger and able to run faster if you need it!" Libby blew through her nose slightly and eased up into a nice and collected but brisk trot.

Boy it was a beautiful day! The sun was coming up so nicely now and the day was settling in to be gorgeous. It was still a little nippy. There was a slight breeze. Liza could see the hills approaching. Then she looked down at the stones on the trail.

She saw fool's gold and other kinds of stones. It seemed every time she turned a corner on the trail there were different kinds of stones. "These stones down here are slightly reddish," Liza said to Libby. "And back just a bit near the huge cactus there were black ones with white in them. I wonder if they are some kind of quartz," she said.

"I bet there were outlaws here at one time, Libby," Liza continued. "Outlaws running up and down these trails with a posse after them. I wonder if we should go up into a lope. Or even a gallop. Would you like to, my girl?"

"Liza," her mother called. "Liza, stay with us."

Liza scowled for a moment and said, "I want to chase bad guys, Libby. Let's go." She knew it was wrong but she loved these trails so much and just wanted to have some fun. Liza also knew her parents could see where she was headed and didn't think they would really mind if the two of them ran on ahead.

Hearing her voice, it was as if Libby understood and she perked up her head when she heard Liza speak to her. So, when Liza gave another squeeze in her legs and made a small kissing sound, Libby immediately picked up the pace and soon Liza and Libby were dashing up the trails. Not furiously. Liza just wanted a little exercise for the two of them. She loved to have fun on the trails whenever they went out together. It was fun to pretend a little too. No, a lot! It was really fun to pretend! And why not? Liza hoped she was never too old for all of this.

"Let's pretend we are chasing bad guys in real cowboy days, Libby! We're part of a posse. Let's go get'm! Ride, Libby, *RIDE, GIRL!*" Liza cried. She was exhilarated and ready to run with her mare.

Libby went up into a lope. Charging forward, her neck and head straight out, tail flying, legs placed confidently on the trail, Libby powered herself and her rider up the hills running on the trails just like she was a mustang.

Liza could feel Libby's powerful muscles underneath her as they zigged and zagged their way up the trails into the highest parts of the hills. Liza had been very wise all these years to keep Libby in excellent shape. For short moments like this, she knew they could have a little bit of fun together, even after a long trip. In her mind, Liza felt that Libby was enjoying all of this too!

Suddenly, almost sharply, Liza cried, "Oh hey, so whoa now girl, whoa," Liza said firmly as she tucked and sat down deeply into her saddle.

Libby slowed her movements pretty quickly almost coming to a skidding halt even though she was on the uphill. "This is odd," Liza thought to herself. The reason for her swift cry of 'whoa' to Libby was evident immediately. Liza and Libby were in a dense fog! "I've never seen fog here in the hills like this before," she thought. "This is very unusual. What is with all this fog here in the hills? I can barely see!"

While Liza knew that these trails didn't exactly drop off dangerously, she also knew that if she guided Libby incorrectly, or if Libby took a stumble accidentally, the tumble off her horse would not be fun and in the fog, too risky. Liza contemplated dismounting. But she stayed on Libby's back a little longer. In spite of the risks, she felt safer to be on Libby. Liza decided to trust Libby's ability to pick her way on the trails, even in the dense fog.

The fog was chilly against her nose and cheeks and hands. Liza wondered if she should pull out another jacket just in case. "But there had been sunshine a moment ago. Where did it go?" she wondered. Liza was confused with this fog and she kept Libby at a confident but cautious walk.

"It's okay girl," Liza said out loud to Libby. "I know you feel comfortable continuing to walk, but I'm a little bit concerned. I've never seen fog like this here in the hills of this part of Arizona."

Libby replied with a confident little whinny.

After a few more twists and turns on the trail, Liza suddenly realized she should have either waited or headed back to her parents. They knew Liza was safe riding on Libby, but Liza felt it was only fair to let her parents know she was okay.

"I want to do the right thing," Liza thought, "but I'm not sure I want to ask Libby to turn around here on the trail.

Perhaps we will go just a little bit further and then we will turn around."

Liza could not see very far in front of her at all, and even though Libby was sure-footed, she definitely did not want to chance turning Libby around on the narrow trail.

Liza never even thought to just stop and wait. Libby was walking carefully, confidently and methodically. She couldn't see much, but she heard the sound of Libby's shoes against the stones of the trail, and she could hear the small squeaks of her leather saddle. They were still climbing a bit. Liza thought about the climbing and realized she did not remember that this part of the trail had so much climbing either.

"So, this is weird. The fog and now the excessive climb," Liza said out loud. "When will we leave this fog?" she wondered.

And just as Liza was turning another corner on the trail, and just as Liza was contemplating whether to stop and wait for her parents, and just as Liza was deciding whether to turn around and head back to her parents, the fog parted.

CHAPTER THREE

LOST

Liza looked around her. Behind them on the trail she had fog. In front of them, they had absolutely stunning and crystal clear blue skies. It was sunny once again.

"This is kind of unusual," thought Liza. "Do I see little white flowers here and some grass?" Liza knew that on this part of the trail, there were no white flowers like these pretty ones and certainly no lush grass.

"Ooooh, there is grass over there! I wonder if she will dismount for one of her little snack times so I can have some grass," a voice said.

"WHAT???" Liza spoke so sharply and suddenly that Libby lifted her head and stood stock straight and came to a halt again.

Whenever Liza reacted like that, Libby would stiffen her body and go on a kind of calm high alert. If Liza felt danger, Libby did too.

"Who said that?" Liza said. "Who wondered about grass?" Liza asked more forcefully.

"Doesn't she know that I asked about that grass over there? Who is she talking to? It doesn't seem like she is talking to me," the calm voice said.

"*WHO SAID THAT*? Mama?" Liza had a frightened tone to her voice now. She sat up higher in her saddle and twisted her body and looked around. No one was near Liza but she did not know who was speaking! Liza kept wondering, more anxiously now, where were her parents? Liza was slightly frightened and she looked back at the fog bank.

"I wonder why she sounds kind of scared? It's awfully nice here. I like the look of those mountains off in the distance. She sure has taken me on a lovely ride this time," the female voice said again.

"Libby, I'm confused and a little scared. I think we should turn around," Liza said to Libby. Liza always spoke with Libby. She often wondered if Libby knew what she meant when she spoke to her.

"I'm happy to just keep going. The fog has lifted and if you want to stop and have a little snack, just send me over there a bit to have some of that grass."

Liza's eyes popped wide open and she leaned down beside Libby's neck, gently pulling on the reins to the right so that Libby's head turned. Liza looked into Libby's eyes.

In a very slow and calm even tone, Liza spoke words she never ever thought she would utter.

"Did you just speak to me, Libby-girl?" Liza asked. There was a tremble in her voice when she spoke.

There was pause. There was a gentler breeze against Liza's skin and she started to have a chill even though the sun was shining now and even though she was no longer scared.

Libby stood very still and looked back into Liza's eyes.

"Yes, I spoke to you."

"What?!?!?!"

"Yes, I did. I spoke to you. I always speak to you, actually."

Liza sat upright and shook her head. She twisted around in her saddle, once again, looking all about. She thought, "Was someone playing a game? Who was projecting a voice out here in the middle of nowhere?"

Liza looked all over and then quickly dismounted. Holding the reins, Liza stepped backward, eyes focused on Libby.

Then Liza stepped forward and she stood very close to Libby. She stood by Libby for a moment, just looking at her, and suddenly she put her arms around Libby's neck. Liza snuggled her hands into Libby's mane and she leaned her cheek against Libby's neck.

"Girl, this is weird. I'm seeing fog on these trails that I've never seen before. I'm seeing pretty flowers on these trails that I've never seen before. I'm seeing grass along these trails that I've never seen before. And I know I'm repeating myself and not making any sense but this is all so unusual. And now I'm hearing a voice and I don't understand why or how this is possible," Liza said anxiously.

Liza said this all out loud as she rubbed her face into Libby's neck and took an intake of breath as she spoke.

She loved how Libby smelled. Today, she smelled like the wind and fresh air and sunshine and joy.

Liza was a sensible girl but suddenly she was nearly in tears. Her heart was pounding. She held her breath.

There was another moment's pause.

"You are hearing a voice because I'm speaking to you," said Libby.

CHAPTER FOUR

THE VOICE

And just then, Liza jumped backwards and fell down smack on her bottom.

Libby looked down at Liza, sitting amongst the flowers.

Liza looked up at Libby. She could see Libby's long nose and her white forehead and her large eyes. They were looking directly at Liza, almost as though they were looking into her soul.

"I always speak to you," Libby said. "It always seems that you are hearing me and the actual words I am saying. But just now is the first time I'm quite certain you are actually hearing me. Did you hear me wondering about grass and you getting down to have a snack?"

Liza tensed slightly and standing up slowly, she stepped back just a little bit and took a good long look at her horse. Liza had a feeling that her world was changing and felt that her life would never be the same after this very moment. She paused, knowing in fact that nothing really would ever be the same again.

She stepped back a few more steps and looked at Libby again and then looked deep into her eyes. Libby had looked forward for a moment, gazing at the mountains and then turned her head again to focus on Liza. Libby was so relaxed she blinked and kind of closed her eyes! Then she opened her eyes. And Libby looked at Liza. And Liza looked at Libby.

Libby said, "I love you, you know." And with that, Liza fell back down onto her bottom again and looked up at Libby.

Libby walked a few steps closer to Liza and dropped her head slightly. She nuzzled Liza gently and exhaled a gentle blow through her nose.

"And you can hear me. You can hear my words now, correct?" asked Libby.

Uncontrollably, Liza burst into tears. They were tears of joy and bewilderment and tears of intense happiness all at once. Then Liza burst out laughing. And she was kind of hyperventilating with the disbelieving breaths of someone who was beginning to realize that she was talking to her horse and that her horse was understanding her and was talking back to her!

They were having an actual conversation!

"My horse can hear me and I can hear her. I can hear what she is saying. *WHAT IS GOING ON?*" Liza practically screamed inside her head to herself.

"Can you understand me, my Libby-girl?"

"Yes."

"Wait, so you can really understand each word I am saying?" Liza asked again.

"Yes, Liza. I have always understood everything, you know," Libby said.

"I just heard you speak. And you can hear me speak. We are actually talking and holding a real conversation with one another," Liza said. "This is unbelievable!"

"Yes, we are, my dear one," Libby said.

"Tell me something, Libby. Anything. Please." Liza looked at Libby with pleading eyes.

"Well, I just told you I loved you. You seemed frightened and concerned and I felt you needed to hear this," Libby said.

"This is amazing! This is wonderful! Woo hoo!"

Liza stood up and dropped the reins. And then Liza began to twirl. It felt silly but she started to twirl and smile and laugh and giggle and flap her arms to keep her balance as she twirled. Liza kept twirling and twirling and in that moment, Libby dropped her head and snuck in a nibble on some grass.

"I don't think you will mind right now if I munch on some of this wonderfully delicious grass, will you?" Libby asked, mumbling a bit because her mouth was full.

Liza felt dizzy when she stopped twirling. But she was full of joy and happiness and wonderment all at once. She wiped away her tears and smiled.

"Not at all. And I think I will do what you wanted me to do which is to stop and have a little snack and wait for Mama and Papa to arrive," Liza said.

Liza unhooked one of the reins and made a loop of it to hang over the saddle horn, and then she let the other one drop to the ground. Libby stepped carefully and munched on grass, avoiding stepping on the rein that was trailing on the ground near her in the grass.

Liza opened her saddlebag and pulled out a few nuts, chocolates and raisins. Papa always called this GORP. Good old raisins and peanuts. "Some people used walnuts in their GORP," Liza thought. As she nibbled on her snack, she realized that any nut would work with raisins and chocolate! Pausing, she took a water bottle out of the pack and had a sip.

"I wonder where Mama and Papa are?" Liza asked. "They weren't that far behind us," she continued. "I should have listened and waited. Oh, wow this is all kinds of strange. I do not recognize where we are. It all looks so unfamiliar. I don't remember ever seeing mountains over in that direction either," Liza said. "And look how tall they are," she added.

"And you never heard me speak out loud either," Libby said. "So, add that to the list of things that seem odd right now."

Liza took a hard look around and looked down at the ground and back out into the distance. "Perhaps we came over and up another trail that I did not see in the fog and it brought us to this place," Liza said.

Liza was a little uncomfortable. As the minutes passed, it did not make sense that her parents had not arrived. Where were they? "Perhaps Mama and Papa turned around in the fog?" she thought.

Liza was usually pretty confident and didn't worry too much when she was on trail rides, especially with Libby.

She knew to avoid certain wildlife and to keep an eye out for danger. She knew that there in Arizona, to watch out for sudden downpours and to avoid getting caught in the wash of a flash flood. Here in this part of Arizona, she knew to watch out for coyotes and bobcats, and she knew to keep an eye out for scorpions, black widow spiders and painful cacti.

But this was all too weird. This was making her uncomfortable. This was all so very unfamiliar. All of her surroundings didn't make sense. Liza just stood there with her snack and her bottle of water.

Libby was calmly eating some grass and did not seem concerned at all. One leg was placed forward as Libby kept her head down to eat. After chewing a bit, Libby shifted and walked forward a little bit more to find even better grass, and placed her other leg out in front.

And yet indeed, Liza's parents did not come into view. More time passed. Libby had eaten her fill and was standing quietly, looking around and swishing her tail from time to time. After a few moments of contemplation, Liza repacked her water bottle and the rest of the GORP, attached the rein back to

Libby's headstall, stepped up into the stirrup and climbed up into the saddle.

Liza decided to head back to find her parents. She asked Libby to turn around on the trail and when she did, suddenly, Liza was shocked at what she saw. Rather, she was also shocked at what she didn't see. The fog was completely gone! And everything back on that part of the trail looked the same as where she was now.

Unfamiliar!

Tall mountains, grass, little white flowers and tall pine trees were everywhere. The mountains in the distance were sharp and high. In fact, the mountains were very high. No cacti in site. No desert flowers.

"What is going on?" Liza thought.

"This does not look like Arizona," Liza said out loud in exasperation.

This did not make sense whatsoever. The fog was gone and all around her was a type of terrain that she did not recognize. She took a deep breath and tried to calm herself.

"Libby, do you know what is going on?"

"Not really," said Libby.

"Well, I'm confused," said Liza.

"While I don't exactly know what is going on, however, I have an idea of what is going on but I would prefer that you and I climb this trail for a better look around before I comment on what I think has happened," Libby said. "I know that was a very long sentence," continued Libby, "but I'm excited to be able to speak like this!" she said and then nickered.

"You're funny, Libby," Liza said.

"I know," Libby said.

Then Liza asked Libby to walk on. They took a trail that seemed quite steep when Liza looked down off the side of the trail, but the trail itself seemed safe enough to walk on while astride Libby.

She contemplated getting off and leading Libby once more, but once again she felt Libby was surefooted for the climb. Libby was confidently picking her way on the trail but she felt Liza tense up in the saddle.

"Liza, dear girl, it's okay. I've got this. This trail feels good to me and I'm a-okay to climb. Don't worry about us here on the trail," Libby said quietly but confidently.

Liza heard Libby's gentle voice but at the same time, she was not fully comprehending why the trails all seemed confusing and so different from her memory. She had ridden here many times before, so what was going on?

"I'm glad Libby is confident. I could use a dose of confidence. And where are my parents?" Liza asked herself.

After a bit of climbing, there was a fork in the trail and Liza had the choice to direct Libby onto a trail that was beginning to head down a bit. They had already climbed up very high and had gone up and over some kind of a mountain.

The views were breathtaking. They reminded Liza of some of the trail rides she had taken in Montana, Wyoming and Colorado. She had been in the Rocky Mountains many times and while this seemed similar, Liza knew this was not Arizona terrain and she had a feeling these weren't the Rocky Mountains either.

There were very sharp and extremely high mountain peaks all around her, and in the distance, evidence of snow. The air was clean and fresh and beautiful. The sun was on her and that gave her a comforting feeling.

The trail began to descend and Liza felt that might be a good thing. They had climbed a fair amount at the beginning of the trail ride. Now it was time to descend.

She still did not see any sign of her parents however.

"I can't imagine that they are lost or that they turned around, but this is very strange. Perhaps they returned to the campsite? Did they go back to the trailer? Or were they lost in the hills like I am? I'm sure they are worried about me, about us. Or did they stop for something and are trying to catch up to me and can't find me? Was it wrong for me to travel forward into this strange land?" Liza wondered.

"Great, now I'm really scared," she said.

CHAPTER FIVE

THE ZING

Anna was in her garden when she felt it. She was bending over tending to some flowers, gently pulling weeds, and moving around some soil to help some of the plants stand up straighter. Her garden was full of herbs, flowers and vegetables. Many of the plants she gathered and hung to dry were both for cooking and for medicinal purposes. Many of the vegetables she ate fresh during the season, and many more vegetables she put up for the wintertime by canning or pickling or drying.

Today, she was diligently working in the garden when she felt something unusual.

Anna paused, and stood up slowly. Very slowly.

"Well that was odd," she thought.

She wiped her hands in front of her to loosen the dirt that was there from her gardening work. Then she rubbed her hands briskly together a little bit more to finish cleaning them. She stood even straighter and she put her hands on her hips. She stood calmly and quietly, contemplating what she had felt.

Anna had felt a zing.

It was definitely a zing.

That was the only way she could describe it. Anna wasn't even sure if zing was a word. But that was what she had felt. It had started in her toes and had run up her legs and through her body like a whoosh. The zing wasn't unpleasant and didn't hurt and neither did the whoosh. But together, both the zing and the whoosh made her feel as though something important had happened.

Anna knew it wasn't her heart and she knew it wasn't her head. This would also be difficult to describe to anyone because a zing and a whoosh almost seem like a medical condition. And Anna would know about medical conditions. As she stood calmly, she pondered and let her mind run through all of her medical training. "No, not that. No, not that either. Definitely not that. Nope. None of those things," she thought, mentally checking off a number of possibilities. Anna was highly trained and highly skilled. She knew what *wasn't* happening to her.

She took one hand off of her hip and then put it up under her chin. She held it there, tipping her head down a tiny bit and scrunching up her mouth in a crooked, pondering smile while furrowing her eyebrows.

"I wonder," she said to herself. "I just wonder. But no, it can't be that. Because I am right here and I never left this spot. I woke up, I washed my face and I brushed my teeth. I dressed and fed the animals. I got breakfast and did some chores and then I came into the garden. I'm right here so it can't be that," she continued, musing to herself.

Anna brushed back a wisp of dirty blond hair that had fallen down. She had loosely tied it into a bun at the base of her neck, fastened with a homemade wooden hair clip-like pin. It usually held all of her hair back securely but bending over in the garden sometimes made wisps of hair fall down into her face.

Anna was wearing a pretty and loose-fitting homemade but expertly sewn cotton dress with beautiful prints on it. There were swirls and flowers and it was full of happy colors. On top of the dress was a well-loved apron that was tied neatly at the back. She had big pockets in her apron, and they were often full of useful things like a small pair of scissors, a piece of string or a button.

Because she was somewhat rebellious, under her dress, she wore a pair of black trousers. None of the other village ladies wore trousers, but Anna did. Anna also wore sturdy leather boots. These were very sensible for a woman like Anna who was very active and climbed up and down the mountains.

On her head, she had fashioned a wide-brimmed hat out of leather and felt to keep the sun off of her face and out of her eyes. She wore pretty earrings that dangled and sparkled in the sunlight. One ear had two earrings and one ear had three. More than one person she met had noticed that combination but none had asked why it was so.

Anna was also a practical woman. And she was thirty-five years old.

Anna was outdoorsy, athletic, feminine, lean and tall. At roughly six feet tall, she nearly towered over most people who she met. She was certainly taller than anyone in the village where she lived. She worked hard with her little farm in the valley and tended her animals with care. She was a strong woman, which helped with all of her chores on her little farm. She had many chores and for the most part, did all of her work by herself. Sometimes neighbors helped one another during haying time. Anna helped others in the village and they helped her.

Everyone in the village knew of the tall woman who had appeared one day and decided to stay and make this village her home. Anna never really spoke much about her past and where she had lived. Most villagers were curious but they were also polite. Anna was a smart, skilled, hard-working and kind woman and those were important qualities in the village.

She lived in her own wooden home nestled there in a peaceful valley surrounded by high mountains. It was three stories tall with a sharply pitched roof to keep snow from piling up too high. The home was a deep, dark-brown, rich blackish color that was well taken care of, yet remained unpainted. In fact, no one painted their homes where Anna lived.

On each floor, at each window, she had window boxes with beautiful flowers tumbling over the sides of them. Anna liked pink and orange and yellow flowers with just a hint of reds. Many of the villagers had red flowers in their window boxes but Anna enjoyed her own color combination.

Anna was young and healthy enough to know that the zing was probably nothing medical. Given her own healthy outdoorsy lifestyle, the more she thought about it, the more she was even more certain that the zing did not mean anything was medically wrong with her.

So Anna was puzzled when she had felt the zing. Yet as she stood there, her puzzlement turned to awe. She stood up straighter. She smiled and yet she became breathless for a moment. So much so that she almost stumbled as she stepped backwards slightly as contemplation turned to understanding.

Anna dropped her hand to her side. Her mouth opened up into a shocked look as she said, "Oh my!"

But she knew that zing. In her heart and soul, she knew it. It was hard to explain, even as her mind raced. She knew what it meant.

"Oh my!" she exclaimed. "A Traveler has arrived!"

CHAPTER SIX

THE BEAUTIFUL TRAIL

Everywhere Liza looked she saw beauty. As she and Libby descended, Liza noticed how the terrain and the flora changed considerably. When she was up high everything was a little bit more barren looking. As she and Libby descended, she noticed the numerous pine trees and more lush, grassy areas everywhere.

"This is very odd," Liza said to Libby. "Arizona doesn't have pine trees where we were camping. So why are there so many pine trees everywhere I look?" she asked Libby.

"Well from my perspective, I love the grasses and I am enjoying the cool fresh air and the sunshine," Libby said. "In fact, I can hear a stream up ahead and would love to stop for a drink if you don't mind."

"Well sure, Libby-girl, absolutely!"

Libby picked up a little trot and headed down the trail and soon enough, Liza could hear the sounds of the rushing water.

"I'm glad you found this stream, Libby," Liza said. The stream was near the path itself and while you could hear the water sounds, it wasn't completely obvious to anyone unless you were really thirsty. Liza was glad that Libby heard the stream.

"I think I will fill my water bottle back up," Liza said.

Liza knew that often times, water from high up in the mountains can be cleaner than water found in other locations. She wasn't exactly sure if it was safe to drink but it sure did look inviting. They had traveled a number of hours on the trail so far and Liza had been taking sips from one of her water bottles. She knew that while it was important to stay hydrated, it was equally important to take advantage of places to refill her water supply, and she was relieved to find the fresh and clean looking water.

Liza dismounted and holding the reins in her one hand, she walked over, bent to the stream and began to fill her water bottle.

Libby followed for a few steps then walked right past Liza and dropped her head down into the water. Liza liked the silly little sipping noises Libby made when she drank water. Liza giggled.

Libby lifted her head and turning to look at Liza she said, "And okay, so why are you giggling, my little one?"

Liza kept giggling.

"Are you laughing at me?" Libby asked.

Liza was giggling and smiling so much her mouth hurt for a moment. She caught herself and tried to look a bit more dignified.

"No, Libby," Liza said. "Not at all, but when you are drinking water, it's funny to watch your lips stick out a bit and to hear you drink the water, so that made me giggle," she continued.

"Okay so maybe I *am* laughing at you," Liza said mischievously.

"Hmmm," said Libby. "Then let me make you giggle some more!" Libby dropped her head again into the stream and began to drink even more water. And then, for just a moment, Libby made deeper, even more pronounced sipping noises and soon, Liza was howling with laughter!

After the sipping and the giggles had stopped, Liza continued to look around her with wonder and awe. She was resigned to the fact that this wasn't Arizona. She had pinched herself a few times so she knew this was the present and it was all very real and was not a dream. She was a logical young lady and yet she was willing to accept that something startling had happened.

She could tell that this was an important moment in her life. She knew she was experiencing something awesome and fantastic. And it was all so unbelievable.

As she had spent more time with Libby these past few hours, Liza had felt a strange calmness come over her. It was almost a dreamy calmness. She knew she should be worried about her parents and where she was, but she had started to feel a compelling sense of adventure rising inside of her. On the one hand, she wanted to have an adventure yet on the other, another part of her felt an urgent need to find her parents and to figure out what had actually happened to her.

Most of all, she was really enjoying this new reality of being able to talk to her horse and to have her horse talk back to her. To actually hold a conversation with your horse, now that was something no one would believe! And that's because Liza could not believe it. She could not believe it was true and over the past few hours had continued to pinch herself to see if this was really true.

She kept asking herself, "Did my horse talk to me? Did I understand my horse? Am I on a mountain that is beautiful and wondrous? Am I on the beginning of an adventure?"

Liza asked these questions of herself over and over and finally said, "Yes, yes, yes and YES! *THIS IS ALL REAL!*"

So over the past few hours, Liza and Libby had been like a happy pair of chatterboxes. Talking and talking and talking and talking. Asking all kinds of questions of one another and learning more and more about one another as the miles went by during their ride. Libby seemed to have boundless energy. Liza felt very energetic as well. Whatever fear she had felt when she came through the fog, well, that was gone now. Mostly gone, that is.

Liza was with her beloved friend. She was with Libby. She felt more confident than she had ever felt before. It almost felt magical, almost otherworldly. Liza felt calm and happy and alert and even though she was taking sips of water, she wasn't feeling very hungry. She knew that was odd, so she made herself have some snacks in case this world she was in was giving her a false sense of energy.

Liza looked around her again and again to see if she could make some sense out of what she saw. Libby had taken it upon herself to go over to have some more grass, so Liza went ahead and removed Libby's headstall and just let her free. Would Libby run away? No. Would some horses run away in a situation like that? Absolutely. But somehow, Liza knew that there would be no reason for Libby to leave her. By removing the headstall, Libby did not have a bit in her mouth and could eat more freely.

Horses always seemed to need to eat. Libby was well exercised, so eating as much grass as she wanted wasn't a problem. Plus, with all this riding around in the mountains, Libby was burning energy too so Liza just let her eat all the fresh grass she wanted.

As Liza looked around her, she thought she saw a trail sign. "Well that is a relief," she thought as she breathed a sigh. "Finally, a sign on these trails. This might all start to make some sense," she thought.

Liza took a few steps down the trail to try to read the trail sign. It was a tall wooden post with a hand carved wooden sign attached to it. Liza was pretty sure it was hand carved. Most trail signs she had ever seen while trail riding were made of dark painted wood with machined grooved lettering, and the lettering itself was painted in white or yellow. That's what a lot of trail signs looked like when she was trail riding with her parents in State Parks or on National Park trails.

She always liked maps and signs. Liza was pretty comfortable reading maps and orienting herself by noticing where the sun was and by looking at landmarks. The trail she was on now, though not wide and groomed, seemed well-used enough. So when she noticed a sign finally, that seemed like a relief. Perhaps she could make some sense of everything now.

As she got closer, she saw an arrow above the sign but there were no words! Instead, there was an ornate circle with carvings all around it forming an intricate yet delicate pattern. It had a rustic look to it and the flowing geometric nature of the carvings made Liza feel comfortable, even though she wasn't certain what it meant.

"Does this mean we go down this way?" Liza asked Libby as she turned to look at her horse. "I mean, there has been no sign of people or animals or traffic or anything all this while. Usually there is an airplane overhead somewhere way up high even if we don't run across any people when we are trail riding. So this is all weird," she said.

"Libby, we aren't in Arizona. This is a fact. I accept that now," Liza continued.

Libby had stopped eating and walked toward Liza. She also looked at the sign, if you could call it a sign.

"Liza, it's evidence that someone has been here and I believe that someone or something is directing anyone on this trail toward them. It's an awfully pretty and carefully made sign, and made with a great deal of care. It's the only thing we have seen in several hours up here so why not let's follow it?" Libby asked.

Liza nodded her head in agreement.

"We have plenty of daylight left that's for sure but I would like to be off of these mountains before the end of the day. I have supplies with me but I don't want to have to camp here," Liza said. "I think we follow this sign. That works for me."

Libby nodded and gave a small comforting nicker.

Liza gave herself a little stretch and put the bridle back on Libby. She checked the cinch and tack, and then climbed back up into the saddle.

And so, they followed the little sign. They did not know where it would lead them. They did not know how long they would have to travel. But Liza felt certain that the sign was made for a purpose and it seemed to have meaning. So they took that turn in the trail and headed down in the direction of the arrow on the mysterious sign.

CHAPTER SEVEN

ANNA'S HOME

Anna made her way back to her home. She put away her gardening tools at the doorway and stepped inside closing the door carefully behind her. It was an old wooden door with heavy metal hinges and strong metalwork for a handle and latch. Inside, there were neat wooden tables and chairs.

The windows were thrown open to let in sunlight and fresh air. Hanging from the windows were dainty, white lace curtains with carefully embroidered designs on them. One set of curtains had horses on them. Anna had made those herself. In another room, there were other curtains with geometric patterns on them, as well as embroidered flowers and animals.

That room was Anna's office. It was full of books and supplies and what looked to be medical instruments. There was a separate door leading to the outside. On one table was a microscope. Propped up nearby was a heavy textbook that was open to a page with medical drawings on it. The book looked heavily annotated in a woman's handwriting style.

Anna's home was neat and clean. It took a lot of work every day to keep her little farm going and to take care of animals, her garden, to dry her herbs and to put up food for the winter. Her kitchen was large and spacious. She had numerous bundles of herbs hanging from the ceiling in her kitchen and in a second room off to the side. These bundles were of vital importance both for nutrition and for healing.

Anna stuck a small piece of wood into the metal cooking stove, stirred up the fire and moved a kettle of water into place on top of the stove. She went to a shelf and pulled down a jar and put a pinch of tea into a nearby cup. Waiting for the water to boil, she selected a small bundle of herbs, pinched off some leaves into her hand, rubbed some into the palm of her hand and added it to the cup.

Out of habit, she deeply inhaled the aroma of the herbs that had been in her palms. They smelled delicious! Then she briskly cleaned her hands by rubbing them together in order to flick off errant herb pieces. Then she sat down and carefully considered her options.

She looked around her kitchen and into the rooms that were set off of the main kitchen area. She contemplated her life up until this very moment when she felt what she felt out in the garden. It had been a very definite zing and a definite whoosh, no doubt about it. She had waited a long time for that to happen again. And now, while working in the sun in her treasured garden, she had felt it. It took a moment, but then she knew exactly what it meant. She just wanted to sit down to contemplate her options and to reflect upon her life.

Anna knew that a Traveler had entered her world.

Every step she would take right now was important. It was important to her and it was important to others. How she reacted to all of this would make a difference to many people and she wanted to react very carefully. She knew that the events of these next few days would have an impact because there was no way a Traveler could enter this world and not make a difference.

She looked at the artwork on her wall. She looked at the wooden furniture, all carefully made. She looked at the carvings on her chairs and she looked at the intricate paintings along the edges of one of her tables. Anna worked hard but she also enjoyed beautiful things. She loved color and designs and beauty and her home expressed those things. Much of what was in her home was handmade, either by herself or by others.

She often traded what she made with friends. She enjoyed that. It meant that her home was filled with the hard work of many people and she really liked that. She liked knowing that what she had made was in the homes of others as well. She looked over at her little studio in the corner. She saw her paints, her woodcarving equipment and her table with a few artistic projects in the middle of it.

Just then she realized the water had boiled. She poured it into her teacup, then sat down again. She ladled out some honey from its container and used another spoon to stir the cup. She took a sip and savored the taste of it.

Enjoying her tea, Anna heard a small noise. It was a small crunching sound actually, and it was just outside.

One of the windows overlooking a pasture was propped wide open especially and Anna turned her head at the sound. A nose carefully inched its way in through the window and then Anna saw a head, with curious ears and loving eyes.

The big buckskin looked over at Anna and said, "I felt it, too, Anna. It's time."

CHAPTER EIGHT

THE TRAVELER

The boy was in the fields on a gentle hillside with the flock of sheep when he saw Liza and Libby coming down the trail.

He hadn't seen many people coming down that trail recently so the movement of horse and rider caught his eye. He turned his head and made a shrill whistle. All the sheep looked up and then looked down and returned to grazing when they realized there was no danger.

Balthazar had made a whistle that could be heard by his younger sister who was closer to the house.

She was with her mother and the cows.

The clang clang clang of the cow bells was soothing. They were walking them down toward the house from another field, and with each step there was a clang or a clung or a ding or a dung. Each bell was made differently so each bell had a different tone. There was a lovely far off melody in the air from the bells. It was beautifully haunting and enchanting all at once.

The boy named Balthazar was actually called Balthis by his family, and when he whistled again, his sister looked up. His eyesight was keen and he saw her looking up at him. He turned and pointed to the horse and rider. He waved at his sister then turned and pointed again. She turned and looked as well.

Then Balthis could see his sister tug at his mother's skirt and he saw his mother look up the hillside at him. Following his outstretched arm, she too looked over at the horse and rider coming down the trail.

The little girl, Meia, was curious. "Mama, we might have a guest tonight!" she cried out.

"Yes, but you never know if a rider from the hills wishes to stay or to press on. There are many miles until they come to a village that might be their actual destination, so don't get your hopes up."

Meia's eyes were pleading. The Mother sighed.

"Yes, my little wildflower. I will ask the rider to stay, of course," her mother said with a smile.

Meia was delighted.

In the distance, Liza also saw the movement. Well, she heard it first. In fact, Libby actually heard it first because for a moment it startled her ever so slightly. Libby lifted her head up at the first hint of the noise of a clang and then the sound of a whistle.

Then Liza had heard it as well, and she soothed Libby who had momentarily begun to spook in place.

"Silly girl," Liza said, stroking Libby's neck, "those are just bells."

"Did you say you are hearing bells here in the mountains?" Libby asked.

"Weellllll," Liza said in a drawn-out manner. Then she paused. "Bells?" she said in a questioning tone. "Bells in the mountains of Arizona? Not possible."

Liza's eyebrows scrunched up a bit as she began to get lost in thought.

"Liza dear," Libby started to say gently, "Liza my dear, we aren't..." but Libby was not able to finish her sentence because Liza had given a little squeeze with her knees and asked Libby to trot a little bit. That part of the hillside was gentle and Liza wanted to move closer to the sounds she was hearing.

Libby held her thoughts and went up into a trot.

As they continued on the path, they went into an area of trees and the cool scent of pine was intoxicating.

Liza took a deep breath and realized how much she simply loved the wonderful scent of pine trees. It was one of her favorite scents in the entire world. Her mother had made some little miniature pine needle stuffed pillows, and Liza kept one by her bedside both at their ranch and in their trailer. Sometimes Liza would crunch the little pillow in her hands and savor the scent. It was an "mmmmmm" kind of scent and as Liza recalled the memory, she perked right up.

Libby picked up her pace a little bit more because she was also excited to see what would be on the other side of this stand of pine trees. She also wanted to understand the meaning of the noises. Especially those bells!

Trotting along on the path, Liza was enjoying the powerful feeling of Libby underneath her. Liza respected every step Libby took and tried to make sure to post carefully in sync with her movements. Up, down, up, down, up, down, post, post, post.

Every good equestrian knew how to post correctly when they were in the saddle. Liza and Libby made it all look so beautiful and professional with Liza's nice posture and soft hands on the reins. And even though Liza was slightly impatient, she stayed calm on Libby's back as they trotted through the little stand of trees.

When Liza and Libby emerged from the trees, Liza looked toward the source of the bells. Lush meadow grass was everywhere. "Now this is truly bizarre," she said.

But Liza was going to be surprised even more. Because right there, out past a little outcropping of stones, was a herd of sheep.

"This is impossible," Liza said to Libby. "Sheep here? Impossible. And with bells on their necks? Why it seems like we are out of a postcard from Switzerland or something. The next thing you will know we will see cows with huge bells around their necks," Liza said slightly impatiently. "No. No, no, no, *NO!* We did not hear cowbells," she added.

Libby stayed silent. Libby did not say one word.

The trail continued on and Liza could now see below that the sheep were being herded down from the hillsides.

She saw a boy in the fields with the sheep and then she realized he was looking at her. She waved. And he waved. He pointed down the fields a bit. Liza brought Libby to a quick stop. She sat down firmly and said, "Whoa."

Looking slightly shocked, a little further away Liza saw the most amazing sight. There was a herd of cows with big bells around their necks.

"Impossible!" Liza said. "What is going on?"

"Liza," Libby said. "You need to listen to me for just a moment," Libby said quietly.

That calm feeling that Liza had had all morning was starting to fade away. For a moment, once again, a slight fear had entered her belly and it started to creep up into her heart and then up into her throat. Liza was having a hard time processing what she was seeing and hearing.

"This can't be," Liza said. "This can't be. What is going on here?"

"Liza, I need you to dismount for a moment and stop being concerned and I need you to look at me for a moment. Please." Libby said this firmly but very gently.

A few moments passed. Libby could feel Liza tense up and then relax. It was as though Liza had made an important decision. Libby felt Liza move in the saddle, turning and looking this way and that. Then Libby felt Liza stop and sit calmly for a moment once again.

After another moment, Liza dismounted and walked around to the front of Libby. Libby bowed her head and nuzzled her nose into Liza's elbow and then into her hand as Liza lifted her hand up to pet Libby.

When Liza and Libby would trail ride together, before they headed out, they often did this. Standing together side by side, one of them would usually lean over to the other for comfort and quietness. Sometimes Liza would lean over into Libby and sometimes Libby would lean over into Liza.

They would do this at competitions too before they were getting ready to go into the arena. The two of them would have a quiet moment together. Liza would speak soothingly to Libby and tell her all the plans for the day. Libby would listen patiently, understanding every word Liza said.

So just now, after many hours up in the mountains, after coming through the fog bank, after the confusion of the fog and the trails and wondering where her parents were, and after seeing the mysterious sign, Liza finally felt like something special was about to happen and she decided to trust Libby and just listen.

"I'm listening, girl," Liza said.

Libby stood there a moment longer while Liza stroked Libby's forehead and then rubbed her mare's cheeks. Libby took a breath and exhaled deeply and audibly through her nose. Liza giggled. Libby was glad to see Liza was relaxing.

Then Libby spoke.

"Liza, my dear, you are about to experience something extraordinary. Are you listening?" Libby said gently.

Liza nodded her head. Her eyes were downcast.

"Liza, it will be hard for me to explain everything to you but the most important thing I can say to you right now is to trust what you will experience and to try not to fight the feeling that something isn't right. Don't fight the fact that something doesn't make sense. Just enjoy the experiences you are about to have and don't try to question everything. Do you understand?" Libby spoke tenderly to her little cowgirl.

Liza was quiet. She nodded her head and she looked up at Libby and then she nodded again.

"Liza?" Libby said in a tone meant to capture Liza's attention.

"Yes Libby. I understand a little bit. Not completely because you haven't explained everything but I think that I just have to trust you and believe that everything is going to be okay. Because today has been such an odd day. It's been a fun day being with you. But today has been odd. Either I am dreaming, which I don't think I am, or this is all very real, which I think it is."

Liza paused a moment and then continued.

"And that means I have to trust you that everything is okay. You are speaking to me. And I understand you. And you understand me. I don't think we are in Arizona anymore. I have a feeling I know approximately where we are but I'm confused how we got here. I have a feeling the fog bank was a part of all of this. And so, I know this is all real, and you are kind of warning me that something more is going to happen and I am going to have to trust you that it will all be okay. Is that correct?" Liza looked into Libby's eyes as she spoke.

Libby seemed to have relief in her eyes. She started to chew with her mouth a tiny bit, with a calm moment of comprehension and wisdom showing in her eyes as she looked at Liza.

"Liza, just enjoy every moment you are going to experience from here on out. Remember when I said I had an idea of what was going on? Enjoy, believe and live and learn. Promise me that," Libby said.

Liza's face brightened. She got excited and had that look of inquisitiveness on her face that Libby loved about her little cowgirl.

"I will Libby. I will! I can do this. I will!" cried Liza.

And with that, she climbed up onto Libby's back and they walked down deeper into the valley towards the sounds of the bells.

CHAPTER NINE

IN THE DRAWER

After a pat on the forehead of her buckskin horse, Anna quickly climbed the stairs to the second floor of her wooden home in the valley. She walked into her bedroom and took a deep breath. It was a comfortable room with low ceilings. There was sensible, locally made furniture in it, carefully made with fine craftsmanship. Most pieces had intricately made wooden carvings on them. The room lacked a traditional closet in it. Instead, there was a large wardrobe in one corner of the room holding most of Anna's clothing.

The comfortable-looking bed was the focal point of the room and the headboard was the most intricately carved of all the pieces of furniture in the room. The bed itself was piled high with goose down feather quilts that seemed to nearly touch the ceiling, they were fluffed up so high. These were needed for the chilly nights in this mountainous village.

Above the windows of the one wall, hung curtains, similar to the ones in the other rooms of the house. The lace curtains draped delicately and framed each window. The windows in this room were larger than in the other rooms. Anna loved bright sunlight and loved to look out into the valley past her garden and the pastures of her animals. She paused for a moment to look at the flowers in her window box. "They need water," she thought, and made a mental note to take care of the flowers.

Anna walked along side of her bed and stood in front of a more ornate piece of furniture. She had found this one on her travels and had it brought here to the village. This was a chest of drawers and it was made of a different kind of wood, not typical of the type found here. The lines of the wood grain were long and patterned and curled in places. The handiwork on this piece looked like it had come from the palace bedroom of a queen. It was smooth and polished. Every piece of wood fit together with perfection.

Anna took a good hard look at this magnificent piece of furniture. She trailed her fingers across the smooth top of the bureau-like chest, admiring the craftsmanship. Then Anna looked at the top of the chest.

There, she had carefully chosen figurines positioned this way and that. Some she had purchased on her many travels. A necklace was laid on a doily in the middle and there were earrings lying beside it. The top of the chest was so polished Anna could almost see her face in it.

She trailed her fingers down the front of the chest and across the first drawer then across the face of the second one and then they finally rested on the handles of the third drawer.

The handles were of a fine metal that was tooled and worked with delicate designs. Clearly the handles had been made by a fine craftsman and Anna knew for a fact that they had been made for a great lady who had once owned this chest. She smiled a knowing smile. This was her favorite piece of furniture.

Then Anna put her fingers under the handles of the third drawer and carefully pulled it out. The handles made a gentle tinkle as they jostled against the rest of the metalwork of the handle.

She took a deep breath and slowly exhaled.

Anna stood for a moment looking at the white piece of cloth that covered the contents of the drawer. Memories flooded through her and she caught herself yearning. She opened her eyes widely and pursed her lips.

"I made that choice," she said to herself. "No regrets, Anna," she said quietly. "No regrets," she said with finality. Then, she brought her fingers to rest gently on the contents of the drawer.

She lifted the white piece of starched cloth. It had a white embroidered design all around the edges of the cloth. There were embroidered horses running on each of the four corners of the cloth and it had a pattern work of swirls and flowers connecting each of the horses. Anna held the cloth in her hands, remembering the many days it had taken her to make this beautiful piece of embroidery. She laid the cloth carefully on the bed and then turned back to look inside the drawer.

She had not looked in here for a very long time and what she saw made her yearn for another time in her life. Because lying there neatly her drawer, was a pair of cowgirl jeans full of jeweled bling decorations, a finely made and decorated western shirt, and a carefully folded leather jacket. In two corners of the drawer, lying on their side, were some high quality and beautifully tooled, gently worn leather boots with spurs. But on top of everything, there was an elegant and finely tooled and decorated leather belt with a large and intricate belt buckle on it. It was a show buckle. Anna thought about the last time she had worn it.

"Top Arizona Cowgirl 1985," it said.

CHAPTER TEN

LIBBY MEETS MEIA

By the time Liza and Libby had made the descent into the little hamlet in the valley, Meia and Balthis were out in the yard. Balthis had put up the sheep and Meia and her mother had taken care of the cows. All the animals were in their pens for the evening. There was a fair amount of noise already. A few of the cows were mooing to be milked and the sheep were being sheep. They simply made noise for the sake of making noise.

Even while the children were getting their milking and other chores done, they kept looking over their shoulders at the girl and her horse. It became evident to them that she was traveling alone, and they saw that she was a relatively young person to be traveling alone.

Meia's mother looked at Liza who calmly walked to the gate of the front yard of their home. The Mother was tall and slim and was dressed in a skirt and blouse with an apron on top. Her long brown hair was tied back under a kerchief. She looked kind and welcoming.

Liza said, "Hello."

"Hallo," replied everyone at the same time.

"My name is Liza," she said. "Hmmm, 'hallo' ... I'm speaking to them in English. I wonder if they understand me?" Liza pondered.

The little girl scrunched up her face and looked up at her mother, confused. She looked back at Liza and then again at her mother and then swung around to look at Liza with a bolt of recognition. "She must be saying what her name is," Meia said to her mother.

So Meia said, "My name is Meia," and pointed to herself. Meia was about nine-years-old Liza guessed. She was wearing a pretty little blue dress with an apron over it. Her white shirt had puffy sleeves and for an active child working with cows she looked remarkably neat and tidy. Her brown hair was in braids and the two long braids were twirled around and connected somehow at the back of her head above her neck to make little hanging braids. She wore a red kerchief over her head tied in the back under her braids at her neck line. Liza thought she looked very pretty.

But, for a moment, Liza was confused. The family seemed friendly enough so she did not feel that she was in any danger. Then she lit up like a Christmas tree when she understood. It was a German dialect but it was German alright. Liza's family had mixed heritage and during her schooling at home, Liza had learned French, German and Russian.

"My name is Liza and this is my horse Libby," Liza said in German, first pointing to herself, then to Libby.

"Ah, you speak 'hochdeutsch'," Meia's mother said to Liza. "High German. You speak High German," she said again in the best German she could muster. She said this matter-of-factly and less like a question.

"Yes, yes, I can speak German," Liza said.

"Thank goodness for all the lessons while we traveled on the road," Liza said to herself. She also thought of her German Aunt who she would see from time to time. Her Tante Helen would come to visit when the family was back at their ranch on the East Coast and they would speak German during dinnertime.

"Have you traveled far?" Balthis asked. Balthis was about Liza's age she guessed. And he was dressed in a form of lederhosen, Liza thought, or something along those lines. She thought about what she had studied regarding the cultures of mountain people from Germany, Poland and Switzerland, and she knew many shepherd boys and others often wore lederhosen to school and while working or playing outside.

She looked at the boy more closely, without staring and surmised that he was wearing a set of clothing for working outdoors and herding his sheep. It was a dark greenish-brown color with straps running up and over his shoulders. He was wearing a long-sleeved shirt, boot-like shoes and he had a felt hat on his head. Liza felt he looked like a version of Robin Hood in his outfit and she smiled. She noticed that his clothing was slightly worn but neat and she could see it had been pressed before it was worn.

"Oh, and my name is Balthis," he quickly added.

Liza was still astride Libby who gave a gentle nicker of hello. It was a quiet and gentle sort of nicker, calm and soothing. Clearly, Libby wanted to signal her approval of the situation to Liza and not use her words with Liza in front of these people.

"Well, yes, we have traveled far. First up and then down this mountain until we saw your sign. At least I think it was your sign. It was a round circle with intricate carvings within the circle and an arrow pointing in this direction," Liza explained.

Libby made her small nicker again. "I wonder why Libby isn't speaking and telling me what she is thinking?" Liza thought to herself. "Oh wait, either people won't understand her or she can't let anyone know she speaks," thought Liza.

"I'm glad you found the sign," the Mother said to her. "Welcome."

"Ma'am, well, you see," Liza added, "my horse and I have really traveled a long distance today. May I stop and visit here, perhaps for the night? My mare is tired and I would like to give her time to relax and get a rubdown. Would that be okay?" Liza asked.

"I'll show her the stable, Mama, may I? Please?" said Meia to her mother.

"Certainly, Meia, and yes, Liza, you are welcome to spend the night here and to take supper with us as our guest," she added.

Liza dismounted and Meia cried out an, "Ooooooh."

"What?" asked Liza.

"Your saddle! It's so different. I have never ever seen anything like this," Meia cried.

Liza was confused for a moment. This entire day had been confusing and she did not know what to say or not say about her day. Frankly, she still wasn't sure what had happened. She had this crazy notion that she had traveled back in time somehow. Certainly, she knew she must have traveled to another location. The German-speaking family solidified that thought in her mind. But where was she exactly? And she just wasn't sure of the day or the month or the year. She hesitated to ask.

"Uh, my saddle. Well yes, I, uh, we... we have traveled far, very far. We are from another place that makes saddles like this. And my clothing is very different too. Where I come from everything is different," Liza said.

"Ooooh," Meia said and went over to pet Libby on the nose. Libby lowered her head and closed her eyes when Meia rubbed first her nose, then her forehead and then her cheeks. "I love horses," said Meia. "I am just learning to ride ours," she said. "I simply LOVE horses," she said again. And then she took Liza's hand and skipped in the direction of an outbuilding that was close to the main house.

As they headed off together, with Libby calmly beside her, Liza thought how lovely it was to be walking to a stable with a little girl who loved horses. Here she was, skipping beside Liza with such joyful enthusiasm. And here was Liza, enjoying all of this, with the horse she loved so much, walking on her other side.

She also knew that it was getting dark and after such a tiring day, she knew she and Libby both needed rest. This seemed like a place they could trust.

Meia's mother smiled and watched them walk away and did not say a word.

"That's kind of funny," Liza thought. "Her mother seems very friendly but she has not asked me any questions. I hope everything is okay. Well, I am not going to worry. This seems like a perfectly safe place. Plus, I have Libby right here and if we need to escape, I can just jump out a window and run to Libby, and we can run away if we need to," thought Liza.

Watching her daughter guide Liza to the stable, the Mother smiled again. "We don't get many visitors," she thought to herself. "It's nice to have a visitor, even one so young. What a curious young girl she is," she continued in her thinking.

"I wonder..." she said out loud.

"This is a wonderful surprise. And wonderful news," thought Meia's mother quietly. She smiled a warm and kind smile as she watched Meia and Liza walk to the stable.

Balthis had started to walk away after observing all of this. He shook his head and said, "Girls." Then he shook his head again. "Girls and horses," said Balthis, with a big exaggerated sigh and a smile.

CHAPTER ELEVEN

SPENDING THE NIGHT

Meia and Liza walked Libby to the stable and untacked Libby together. They removed her bridle and hung it and the reins on a wooden peg on the wall. They took off Libby's bell boots that were wrapped around down near her hooves. Then they unwrapped the special support boots that Liza kept around Libby's lower legs, and put both sets of boots on a nearby shelf. With all of the climbing on these mountain trails, they were really protecting and supporting Libby's legs.

They unbuckled and removed Libby's leather breast collar and also hung it on a wooden peg. Then they took off the saddlebags and unhooked the cinch and the back cinch, then removed the saddle and the pad and placed it all on a wooden rack near Libby's stall.

The two girls were like chatterboxes with many conversations about horses and riding. Meia was becoming very attached to Libby it seemed and Liza noticed how the young girl was paying close attention to how to care for her mare. Libby had that effect on people. She was the kind of horse you wanted to pet and that you wanted to take care of and ride and have adventures together.

And Liza never minded that other people loved Libby. She was always happy to teach others about horses!

As Liza put the last of the packs and tack away, Meia found a brush and began to curry Libby. Liza saw that it was kind of rough looking but she knew Libby would not mind.

"Make sure you get the saddle area, Meia. Libby will really like that," said Liza.

"I sure will," said Meia.

Pointing to another side of the stable, Liza noticed some dried hay and grasses. "Is this where I can find some hay for Libby tonight? Would that be alright to take some?" asked Liza.

"Yes, for sure. That corner of the stable is where we keep some hay on hand for the animals that need to spend the night inside," said Meia. "The rest we store up above out of the way and away from varmints. It's also protected from any snow that might sneak into the stable," Meia explained.

Liza looked all around her at the tools, at the peg and groove construction of the stable and at the way the hay was stored. Liza admired how nicely everything was arranged in the stable area itself. Then she looked at Meia's clothing and the way she had her hair braided. Liza also looked out past the stable up into the mountains, which were still visible against a skyline that was colorful even with the sun far down behind the other mountains.

"This really does feel like the Swiss Alps," Liza said to herself.

Libby looked quickly at Liza and for a moment, Liza felt that Libby had heard what she was thinking.

"I really feel like we are in the Alps, but I wonder what time period this is? It seems quaint what I am seeing here, and it looks a little old-fashioned. When we went through the fog bank, did we go back in time in addition to going to another country?" Liza wondered.

Liza knew that Libby was still looking at her so she made a funny face at Libby and then scrunched her nose and made a little giggle. Then she thought, "Does my horse also know geography too?" Libby nickered loudly and snorted with a blow out her nose, the way horses do sometimes.

"Well good night, girl. You will be safe and happy in here from the looks of things," Liza said. She slid a wooden board into place behind Libby, now tucked into her spacious stall for the night. "I will see you in the morning!"

Libby had a mouthful of hay and for a moment, Liza thought she heard Libby say, "Mmmmmpf." Liza smiled.

Meia took Liza's hand and practically skipped with her once again back up the path to the house. "Mama will have something for us to eat before bed. It's very late but I'm sure she will want you to have something at least," Meia said to Liza.

Liza's stomach was grumbling. It was a loud sound too! She sure was hungry.

And she thought to herself, "Am I actually walking up to spend the night in a chalet? This has to be a chalet. I'm pretty sure of it. This is odd but I'm going to enjoy this experience. And wow! This is really quite the amazing day I'm having," Liza said to herself with great determination.

Once inside the chalet, and Liza was certainly even more convinced it really was a chalet, Liza was amazed once again at how neat and tidy everything was. She noticed the comfortable but modestly sized space of the wooden home. It was sensibly laid out with handmade wooden furniture including chairs, tables, buckets, and kitchen tools being used or hanging throughout the interior. Like many families, Meia's mother had a place in the kitchen where she kept herbs and other plants drying, that hung from pegs attached to beams in the ceiling.

"Would you like some hearty meat and vegetable soup and some bread, Liza?" Meia's mother asked her.

"Yes ma'am," Liza said. "I am very tired and if it's alright, may I have just a little and then go straight to bed?"

"Certainly, dear," the Mother said. "Meia can show you where you will sleep and will give you some water to wash your hands and face."

Shortly thereafter, Liza found herself snuggled under a comfortable, thick, but feather light down comforter with a starched cover on it. There were embroidered flowers all along the edge of the comforter cover. She was hunkered down in a bed with large square pillows on it. They were *HUGE*! Liza flomped down again and could not believe how relaxed she was.

Meia and Balthis had shown her where to wash up and while Balthis had his own room, Meia slept in with her mother that night, as she often did when their father was away. So Liza had Meia's room to herself.

"I can't believe that I have gone back in time, and that I am probably in Switzerland, and that I am with Libby who can speak to me and that I am lying in the attic loft of a Swiss chalet up in the Alps," Liza thought all at once. Her mind was tumbling over itself in confused excitement.

But then her mind turned to her parents and how worried they might be. "I can't think about that right now," Liza thought. "I have to stay positive. We came through the fog bank and tried to go back but the fog was gone. And so, we are here and this is where we will stay until we can find a way back home. At least I have met some very nice people and I have Libby and I have supplies. We will be alright, I just know it," she thought as she made a mental note of it all.

This was her last thought of the evening. She was nestled down deep into the pillows with the comforter on top of her and within minutes of hitting the soft pillows, she fell sound asleep.

The next morning, Liza was surprised to find that her clothes were cleaned and ironed and lying over the chair that was in the corner of her room. "The Mother must have spent all night on this, or else I have been sleeping for a long time," Liza thought. It was daylight and Liza could hear that the household was awake. She did not hear a booming voice of a father, so she presumed it was just the children and their mother for now.

"I can't be a total lazybones," Liza thought and she sprang out of bed.

Dressing, she came down the ladder from the loft and immediately went to the Mother to thank her for her clean clothes.

"How may I help you this morning, ma'am? Are there chores?" she asked the Mother.

"Do you know how to milk?" she replied.

"Why yes I do!" Liza exclaimed.

"We have two milk cows in the stable next to Libby. You and Meia can milk those this morning."

Meia took Liza's hand and picked up a bucket and said, "Come with me! Grab the other bucket first. Then let's go to the stable and feed Libby and the two cows we keep there and we can milk both cows at the same time," she said.

As they walked to the stable, Liza noticed all the rows and rows of vegetables and flowers that were growing in the mountain garden that was near the chalet. They walked past the garden that was lined with rustic but neatly installed sticks with woven pieces in-between to create a barrier for any animals that might want to come in and rob the garden of its bounty.

Looking off into the distance, Liza saw meadow wildflowers of all colors. Blue flowers, white flowers, yellow flowers and red flowers dotted the fields. There were many butterflies and birds flying about, and she could hear birds calling to one another.

Occasionally, she thought she heard the shrill whistle of what she imagined might have been the Swiss version of a Southwestern U.S. marmot.

"Are they called marmots here?" Liza wondered to herself. "And oh, the smell of the pine trees! It's heavenly," she thought.

"Good morning Libby!" Liza said.

Libby nickered before they had even seen one another. Liza marveled at how Libby always knew the specific sound of Liza walking into a barn or towards her pasture or towards her stall even before they had seen one another. Libby always made these lovely "hello" horsey sounds to Liza. And now that they were speaking to one another with words, Liza felt comforted by Libby's horsey noises too.

Picking up a special pitchfork, she cleaned the back of Libby's stall and cleaned the stalls of the two milk cows. "Moo," Liza said. The two cows just looked at her. "I guess they aren't talking cows," Liza concluded with a grin.

Meia and Liza freshened up the water buckets of the animals, gave them some grain and tossed them some fresh hay.

Meia brought down two three-legged wooden stools which were hanging on the wall of the stable. "These two cows give us the most milk. We make many kinds of cheeses from their milk and lots of butter too. Mama and I take most of it all down into the village to sell to the villagers who don't have their own cows. Sometimes we take the train from our village to other villages. The train is new for us here. We never had trains before," Meia said casually as she went to work milking her brown and white cow. "I love trains," she added.

"Trains are new here?" Liza asked herself, somewhat confused.

As Meia spoke, Liza was already milking her cow. Liza had spent time on her grandparent's farm back East and had learned how to milk cows by hand even though their operation was automated. Squirt, squirt, squirt went the milk into the bucket, as Liza got into the rhythm of milking.

"Start from the top of the teat and roll the fingers into one another in a downward, gentle, but firm pressure until they come together and the milk squirts out," Liza recalled from her lessons with her grandmother. Liza's movements must have been alright because her cow wasn't complaining. Her cow was chewing and standing quietly.

"This is fun," Liza said to Meia.

While Liza milked, her cow kept chewing on her hay and occasionally lifted a leg to stomp away a fly or two. Otherwise she stood quite still.

"Trains are new here?" Liza thought again, now clearly very puzzled. "How is that possible? Trains are everywhere. What does she mean that trains are new? How can that be? If that's true, then Libby and I have traveled a long way back in time, that's for sure." Liza scrunched her forehead and tried hard to think when trains were first introduced into faraway places like the Alps of Switzerland.

Once the girls had finished with the milking, and after they both rubbed and petted Libby, they went back up to the house with the pails of milk and set them in the kitchen. Then they went back outside and over to a large woodpile located beside the chalet.

Following Meia's example, Liza helped her to bring more wood into the chalet. This was easy work for Liza. She took pride in her ranch chores that she would do back home, as well as all the chores she needed to do when she was on the road with her parents and the horses. After moving the wood to where it was needed, she helped Meia carry buckets of water to various places around the chalet. They brought water from the well to the area near a clothesline. They brought water into the kitchen. And they brought water down to the animals to replace the water they had already given to Libby and the cows. They used a hand pump to fill water troughs for the sheep and the rest of the cows.

Liza noticed that Balthis had already gone up into the hillsides with his flock of sheep. She could hear the noises of their little bells and could see him off in the distance with his flock. There were so many of them! Liza was sorry that she did not get a chance to ask him how he kept them all in line and to understand why they didn't scatter.

Suddenly, Liza heard the sounds of a horn blowing, at least that is what she thought she heard. She stopped and listened again and realized that indeed, it was a horn. She heard its long deep wail. "It has to be an alpine horn," Liza said to herself. "Those are the very long ones that rest on the ground as the musician blows into it," she thought, remembering her studies of Switzerland. Then she heard another and then another. Listening again, she realized that those horns had a soulful tune to them. Even though they were most certainly far away, she could hear them quite clearly.

"Alpine horns are real!" Liza realized. "Of course they are! I learned about them," she said to herself. "This has to be Switzerland," she thought incredulously.

"Meia, is there trouble or are the horns being played for music?" Liza asked Meia.

"We call them alphorns and Papa plays them too," Meia said. "It's quite a pretty sound. Sometimes we use them to communicate up here in the mountains but mostly it's to play something pretty for others to hear," Meia continued. "This is for music today! They often blow them around this time of day."

"Then it's all true. Switzerland it is! It's incredible but Libby and I are in Switzerland!" Liza said to herself again. "But what time period?" she wondered, as she furrowed her brow.

After a few moments, Liza became curious. She was completely convinced she had traveled to Switzerland when they went through the fog bank. Now she needed to know what time period she was in.

"Meia, does your family have any newspapers or something like that here in the chalet?" Liza asked.

"Let's ask Mama," she replied and Meia ran off to her mother to ask.

As Liza came toward the Mother, she nodded for Liza to head to the kitchen table and then said, "First, please have breakfast but as you can see, I already laid out some newspapers for you. I thought you might want to know," she said to Liza.

There was something curious about the Mother. She seemed very casual about the newspapers and Liza thought it was odd that she had made a point of laying them out for her. "I guess she likes staying up with current events too," Liza thought.

Liza had many books at home and she always had some with her when her family went on the road with their horses. The family enjoyed reading about as much as they loved being on horseback. Liza had all kinds of books and she especially liked books about history and books about other countries.

Meia's mother had laid out bowls of yogurt with muesli on top. In the center of the table was some fresh bread and butter and jam. On a cutting board was some fresh cheese and some aged cheese. Liza noticed the little vase of fresh flowers there in the middle of the table. "Mama does that too," Liza thought, "even when we are on the road. She always finds wildflowers for a little vase for our table," she thought again somewhat wistfully.

"I wanted to thank you again for my clean clothes," Liza said to the Mother. Suddenly, her eyes shot open wide. "What if she noticed something strange about my clothes even more than what they all noticed when I first arrived? Surely, she saw the tags inside and she must have questions," Liza thought. "And why hasn't she said anything?" Liza thought again.

After cutting a piece of bread and covering it with butter and blackberry jam, at least she thought it was blackberry, Liza casually slid her hand over to the small pile of newspapers lying on the table beside her. Liza was trying to remain nonchalant and trying to calm her curiosity at the same time. The words were all printed with an older style of typeface, full of serifs and ornate capital letters, she noticed. Reading it in German was a challenge but not impossible.

Meia's mother was near the sink and was cutting the vegetables very methodically. Liza could tell she was watching Liza out of the corner of her eye.

"Statue of Liberty arrives in New York Harbor, a gift from France," one large headline read. Liza widened her eyes and shook her head. Did she just translate that sentence correctly?

"What!" her mind nearly screamed. "'Arrives' … 'a gift' … what?!?!"

She hadn't even looked at the date of the newspaper because the headline was so shocking. Liza looked up at the Mother and then looked back down to the page. Slowly her eyes traveled up to the top of the newspaper and Liza saw the date.

Liza shook her head again. She noticed that the Mother kept cutting vegetables and was busying herself at the sink area. Liza felt that the Mother was not looking directly at Liza on purpose.

"I'm in the 1880's," Liza cried out in her head. "The 1880's!!"

Her head screamed, "How is any of this possible??? So many things haven't happened yet in the world. That's why Meia was talking about trains being just built here in the Alps. We are living in the 1880's!" she thought. "I'm not even born yet. My parents aren't born. My grandparents aren't born yet. How is this possible? This isn't a dream. This is real! Okay, cowgirl, breathe. Just breathe. It's just like you are going into the arena for an important competition. Breathe in, breathe out. Breathe. It's okay. Libby told me I would experience unusual things and to just enjoy everything and learn from it all! So that's what I will do!" Liza finally told herself.

Meia had been chattering away and finally Liza heard what she was talking about. Liza realized Meia was asking her mother if she could take some time today to go riding on Libby, if Liza didn't mind.

"Of course," Liza said excitedly. "Let's get you riding on Libby!"

Liza finished her breakfast and after helping to clean up inside and helping with a few more household chores, she and Meia went back out to the stable. At one point the Mother had given Liza a warm smile but Liza noticed that she still said nothing much to her, other than kind motherly-type pleasantries.

Being with Meia and Libby sure was going to be a nice distraction from what she had just learned about her present situation!

Liza was incredulous about it all. But what could she do? Here she was and that was that.

Liza's mind was a blur. She wanted to have some private time with Libby but that was out of the question. The rest of the morning was spent with a mixture of helping Meia ride Libby, working in the garden, cutting more hay and grass, and helping the Mother to preserve different foods. Liza absorbed everything she could. In her world, they canned foods too but it was much easier with mechanical aids and electricity. Here, it was a world back in time, literally, and everything was done by hand using a woodstove. Liza was enjoying herself and also proud that she could help this wonderful family who was being so kind to her and to Libby.

At one point, the Mother and Liza hooked Libby to a little cart to move a big pile of logs from one area of the little farm closer to the house. The Father was gone with their main horse and when asked, Liza felt it would be fine to use Libby for farm chores. Libby didn't seem to mind.

Every time she was close to Libby, she desperately wanted to tell her what she had learned. Switzerland in the 1880's! This was impossible and yet it was possible.

Because here she was! But all day, Liza had no private time with Libby, so that important conversation would have to wait. Liza's head was simply bursting!

After a hearty lunch, they also tended to some cheese wheels in the cold storage cellar area that the family had. Liza had never seen such large wheels of cheeses and was impressed with all the work and care required to run this farm.

Throughout this day of chores, farm work and fun with Libby, there had been good food and plenty of excellent camaraderie. Liza was glad that Meia had gotten a ride on Libby, and all day she could not stop her excited comments on how much she loved to ride! The day continued with some more work and then suddenly Liza realized as dusk approached, that her day with the family was coming to an end. She was a hard worker at home but this farm life was really hard. She had a deep respect for this little Swiss family.

With darkness almost here, Liza realized that Balthis was back down from the hills with the flock of sheep and that he had put them in the corral that was specially made for them. As he fed and cared for them, Liza and Meia took care of Libby and the two milking cows.

Coming up the road, Liza saw a man on horseback and when he whistled, Liza saw Meai and Balthis stop their chores and run down the road toward him. His whistle was a cheerful one, like a tune from a song, and the sound of it got the children all excited.

"This must be the Father," Liza thought. The sound of the whistle seemed a lovely way for him to announce to his family, "I'm home and I have missed you!"

Liza watched as the man jumped off his horse, and then hugged the children. "That's definitely the Father," Liza thought. She could hear the children chattering and then saw them point in her direction. The Father waived and gave a hearty 'Hallo' to Liza. She waved a greeting in return.

With all of the excitement, the Mother had poked her head out of the chalet and waved to her husband. The Mother had been in the garden picking fresh foods for dinner and must have passed through the kitchen and back outside to greet him. Liza was certain she saw the Mother blow a kiss to welcome the Father because she saw his face light up with happiness.

Then she asked them all, "Children, after your father brings the horse to the stable, carefully tend to the horse. It's been a long week for him so curry him well. When you are finished with your chores, all of you come in to eat."

CHAPTER TWELVE

DINNER WITH A FAMILY

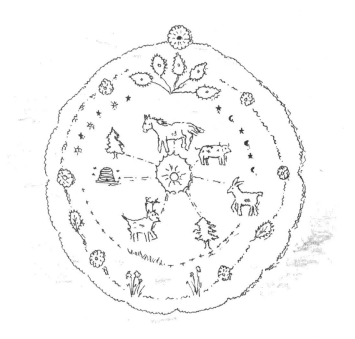

"This food is very delicious," Liza said. "And it all smells so good!" she added.

The evening meal consisted of a hearty meat pie loaded with vegetables. Perhaps the meat was some kind of wild game found here in the mountains. Liza could not decide what kind of meat it was exactly but it sure was delicious. In fact, she decided it was yummy.

"Why thank you very much, Liza," Meia's mother said, acknowledging Liza's compliment. "I'm glad you are enjoying it."

Liza noticed that the cloth napkins had been rolled into long rolls. She also noticed that each napkin was secured by a carved, wooden, circular ring. This, like many things in the home, had been intricately carved and had a lot of detail. Liza noticed a beautiful clock on the mantelpiece that was also ornately carved. It was in the shape of a bear and the bear was in a bed of wooden flowers. His arms seemed to hold the clock timepiece that was embedded in the wooden carving itself. It was stunning.

"I am a woodcarver," Meia's father said. "Some wood-carvers take over their homes with all of their tools and supplies, and the wood chips accumulate everywhere. I have a small hut behind the house next to the stable where I do my work or else it would make a dusty mess all over," he chuckled.

The Mother agreed.

"Father is very good," Meia said. "A prince bought some of his work you know!" she said proudly.

Meia's father had been out and away from home and had returned to his family after nearly a week away. Liza could see that he loved his family very much. His smile was broad and deep. He looked at each member of his family with affection and was curious how their week had been while he was away.

Then the Father turned to address Liza. He said, "I see you are looking at the clock up there on the mantelpiece."

When he was outside, Liza had seen his dark felt hat with a long feather in it and noticed he had worn a heavy jacket and what seemed to be some kind of thick felt or canvas type pants. His boots were dark-brown leather and had a unique style to them. Liza already noticed that the hat and jacket were neatly hanging on pegs in the kitchen near the back door. He was a kind looking man and reminded her of her father.

Liza tried not to feel homesick again, so she looked back at the woodcarver.

He was taller than she expected and must have smoked a pipe with delicious smelling tobacco because he smelled sweet. He had large hands that had definitely seen much hard work in his life. And yet Liza was looking at some woodcarvings that looked like they had been carved by someone with great patience and care and with a skilled hand. She looked again at the bear clock on the mantelpiece.

The Father tousled Meia's hair with loving affection.

"The clock is beautiful," Liza said.

"I travel down into the villages and deliver my carvings to men who then take them into the larger cities to sell for me," the Father said. He looked at his wife and smiled. "Sometimes this work takes me away from my family for a few days at a time or even for a week, but people really like my woodcarvings and the things I make are in high demand," he continued.

"And yes. My work caught the eye of a prince and I was fortunate to receive several more commissions from him," the Father explained.

"Speaking of beautiful, I was looking at your saddle in the stable when I returned home a little while ago," he said, looking at Liza.

Liza stiffened.

"I don't think I have ever seen anything like it," he continued. "It's very unique. Very detailed. And I've also noticed your boots, because they are unusual," he added. "So are your spurs."

Everyone at the table looked at Liza. It got rather uncomfortably quiet for a long time. Liza almost started to count the seconds of silence.

"Darling, I think by now you know that our guest is a Traveler," Meia's Mother said, raising her eyebrows knowingly when she looked at her husband.

Liza scrunched her face and thought, "A 'Traveler'? Why the particular emphasis on that word?"

And before the Father could say another word, his face relaxed and he smiled more warmly. In fact, his was a knowing kind of smile. And then he said, almost bursting out the words, "A Traveler! From the mountains? Ah yes! A Traveler! Of course, of course. Welcome! I'm sure my family kept you busy today, and you must be tired from your journey, so I apologize for all of my questions. Travelers are most welcome here. We are so happy to have you and your mare staying with us," the Father said.

"What's a 'Traveler'?" Liza thought again. But the Father was so happy that she neglected to ask him to clarify his words.

Soon, Liza relaxed quite a bit over all of this. She was happy here but still remained a little bit nervous. She pretty much figured she knew where she was geographically right now and she remained in calm shock at how far back in time she and Libby had traveled. "The 1880's," she said to herself for about the hundredth time.

All of this made her feel both worried and exhilarated at the same time. "But what do they mean by 'Travelers' and do they really know all about me?" Liza asked herself. "And did I translate that word correctly, 'Traveler'?" she thought. "I wonder, are 'Travelers' people like myself who came here from another place and time?"

While Liza was mulling everything over, she saw that the parents exchanged a knowing glance between them.

"Thank you for admiring my saddle and all. I do come from far away and where I live, this is what we use," Liza said. She decided to keep the explanation very simple. If they knew something, she would wait until they revealed more. If they didn't really know all about her, she would not go and make the visit uncomfortable by bringing up the unusual fact that she and Libby had traveled back in time through a fog bank from the mountains of Arizona. Who would believe such a story anyway?

"Indeed, no one has anything like that around here," the Father continued and then nodded and smiled at Liza and his entire family. "We are very fortunate to have you here Liza, and we can learn a lot from you, I'm sure. Children, spend as much time as you can with Liza and learn what you can from her."

Liza wasn't sure exactly what this meant but she was very glad that the topic had moved away from the discussion of her saddle!

Quickly trying to change the subject, Liza took a piece of bread and spread it with some fresh butter that was from a small ceramic bowl on the table. "It's probably from one of the cows I milked today!" she thought. She ladled a bit of a red jam onto it and spread it with her knife. "This is all very delicious," she said. She did not recognize the berry. "Is this some kind of currant?" she thought.

This morning she had tasted a kind of blackberry jam. This evening, the jam was from some kind of currant. She loved jam so she made a mental note to learn how to make it if she ever returned home to her parents again.

After dinner, the family did some chores and Liza took a moment to go down to Libby to quickly check on her for the evening. This was the first moment alone with Libby all day and Liza was simply dying to talk to her!

"Hello, girl," Liza said. Libby was munching on fresh hay and was making chewing noises just like the two milking cows did who were in the stable next to her.

"Libby, I have something to tell you," Liza said.

Libby kept eating.

Liza played with Libby's mane and twirled some of it in her fingers. She absentmindedly began a little braid in Libby's mane and then undid what she had started.

"Well, we had a good day today with this family. The Father has come home tonight and is a very smart and kind man. It's obvious he loves his family very much," Liza continued.

Libby picked up another mouthful of hay.

"Girl, well, you told me something wonderful was going to happen and you were right," Liza added. "They gave me some newspapers and I was looking at the dates and all, and, well, I mean to say, well..." Liza paused.

"Let me interrupt you, Liza," Libby said. "Remember first and foremost that I did tell you this is going to be a lot of fun," Libby said. "Now, so do you think that you have it all figured out? We are Travelers! Right? Is that what they told you?" Libby asked.

Liza was petting Libby on her neck and then stopped and looked at her and said, "Yep. They called me a 'Traveler'. They are a very friendly family and I'm guessing we aren't the first Travelers they have ever met. That's got me very interested. They did not seem worried or concerned that we are who we are, so I have decided not to be worried or concerned about it either. I think we should have fun and have some adventures and enjoy our time here!" Liza said to Libby.

"I think that would be a great idea, Liza!" Libby said. "Now you go on inside. Everything will be just fine. Go have a nice evening. I expect we will be leaving tomorrow, so go enjoy yourself. I have my new friends here in the stable, including the Father's horse who actually seems like a good gelding. His name is Marcel, you know," Libby said. "No one can speak, of course, so we just eat and make nice noises to one another."

And with that Libby shook her head in the exact same way that a dog shimmies and shakes his body after it's gotten wet. Libby shook her head back and forth, which shook her neck all about and finally, shook the rest of her body all over. Her mane and tail flopped about when she shook. Then she made a nicker and a gentle blow through her nostrils that was full of contentment and satisfaction all at once.

Liza said good night to Libby and to the other animals in the stable, and headed back up to the house. Even though the other animals didn't speak, she felt she should say good night to them too.

As she walked up the path, she realized she didn't know what the family did in the evenings and she wasn't sure if she should be preparing for bed or not.

When she came inside, Balthis was at the kitchen table reading a book, and Meia was in a wide chair reading a book of her own, with a little help from her mother who sat beside her. The Mother had a few sewing and embroidery projects in her lap as well, Liza noticed. The Father was smoking his pipe and it smelled delicious. The apple scent reminded Liza of her grandfather and the weekends she had spent with her grandparents.

Liza's grandfather was a watercolor painter and had become quite the renowned artist. In the evenings, he would sit down at his tilt-top easel and he would paint. He painted horses and flowers and all kinds of beautiful things. There was that homesick feeling again, and Liza pushed it aside.

"Oh, Liza, I have something for you," the Father said. He excused himself from everyone and went over to his desk. He had a writing desk in the corner of the main room. There were piles of papers and Liza's guess was that this was where all the important things for his carpentry business were kept.

During the day, Liza had also learned that the Mother sold many food products that she made as well as handmade embroidered items, so her papers were probably in that desk too. "This is an industrious family," she realized.

Walking over to his desk, the Father picked up a small object and held it in his hands. Then, he held it in only one hand and looked at it thoughtfully. "Yes," he said, "she will need this," he said almost imperceptibly.

"This is for you, Liza," the Father said.

Turning to Liza, he handed her the object. He held it first with reverence and then almost hesitated before he placed it in Liza's outstretched hands.

When she felt it in her hand, Liza felt a shimmer of energy in the room. She noticed that all the windows were closed so she knew it wasn't a breeze. She noticed the fire in the fireplace wasn't flickering differently, so it wasn't a back draft either.

And yet she had definitely felt something. It was invigorating and wondrous all at once.

Resting in her hand was a small circular piece of wood with a small hole in the top into which was tied a supple leather string that looked very sturdy.

"I will take very good care of this gift," Liza said. Something inside Liza told her that this was a very special object. She looked at it in awe and as she continued to hold it, she felt the energy again.

She was looking down at the beautiful circular disk in her hand as she spoke. She observed that it contained some of the most delicate and intricate woodcarving she had ever seen in her young life. The larger carvings in it contained circular geometric patterns with swirls and designs. The whole thing had the appearance of a talisman.

But the more she thought about it, Liza realized that this gift almost seemed heavenly, and it definitely seemed otherworldly. It was three-dimensional of course, and she gracefully ran her thumbs then each of her other fingers all over it. The tactile sensations were electrifying.

As she examined the patterns in the disk, a memory shot into her head.

"This looks exactly like the wooden sign up the trail closer to the woods that Libby and I saw the other day!" Liza realized.

"Hidden in this design, does this contain the name of this chalet? Or is this just a symbol of their chalet or something?" Liza wondered about that for a moment.

"Or does it have a deeper meaning?" she pondered.

Liza felt a warmth emanating from the carving and the entire experience felt very special, and so she held it even more carefully.

"I will take very good care of this," Liza said again. "It's quite beautiful. But I'm afraid I don't have anything to give to you in return," Liza continued.

"Your visit has been enough," said the Mother. "My children have enjoyed meeting you and I know my daughter has enjoyed her time with you. And you have been very helpful today, and Libby certainly helped quite a bit too!" The Mother's compliments made Liza smile.

Liza put the wooden gift into her pocket.

Soon the evening chores were done and the house was quiet with everyone tucked in their beds. Meia had stayed in a trundle bed in her parents' room again and so Liza had Meia's bedroom all to herself.

Liza could not sleep.

Instead, she climbed out of bed and walked to the window. Looking out, there in the moonlight she could see the stable against the outlines of the pine trees in the background and she could make out the Alps themselves in the distance. Liza thought of the animals safely tucked in for the evening, either in their pens or in their stalls.

As she looked at the moon and the moonlit landscape, Liza thought about all the many experiences she had already had here with this family. She thought about her own family too. She missed her parents.

But she felt that she was taking part in a very special adventure right now. She and Libby had taken trails up and down mountains and had taken this particular trail which led them to this valley and to this family.

Where would they go after this? And what would happen next for them?

She could not wait to talk to Libby in detail about everything that had happened and she was certainly eager to hear what Libby really thought about all of this.

And as soon as she climbed back into bed, and as soon as she got all snuggled into the fluffy pillows with the fluffy comforter on top of her, Liza fell fast asleep.

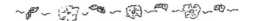

CHAPTER THIRTEEN

THE BUCKSKIN

Anna walked into the pasture wearing everything she had found in the drawer. She loved the feeling of being in her cowgirl jeans again and she really loved the feeling of pulling on those comfortable western boots of hers.

The buckskin had been enjoying some grass and lifted her head. Abby had heard Anna walking into the pasture and from the corner of her eye, had seen what Anna was wearing.

The buckskin also noticed that the door to the tack shed area was open and that leather packs and a bed roll were lying there on a table next to the shed. Anna walked confidently yet casually and headed to the shed where she kept Abby's tack. Or was she headed to the pasture? Abby couldn't tell.

The buckskin quickly lowered her head and then kept her head down to eat. She strained to watch Anna. This was Anna's moment and she didn't want to ruin it for her. Then the buckskin lifted her head again and looked right at Anna when Anna came to a stop in front of her.

"Well, Abby, it's time, just like you said. I think you felt it too," Anna said to her horse.

"I did. You know I felt it. But I left you alone to figure out what you wanted to do about it," Abby replied.

"Another Traveler has come and my sense is that we should help her," Anna said.

Abby was thoughtful and tossed her head. There was a breeze and her mane was caught in the breeze as she tossed her head a second time. She looked magnificent.

"I knew I wasn't the only one, you know, so this is exciting for me too," Abby said casually, as she lowered her head once again for a mouthful of grass. She took a slow step forward, placing one hoof in front of her nose as she swirled her lips, catching grass in her teeth, and then eating it. She kept her head down, knowing that Anna was looking at her.

"Well you were right all along," Anna said. "I should have really listened to you a while back when you said that more would come," Anna continued. "They probably got in the same way we did, don't you think?" Anna asked her mare thoughtfully.

Abby's head shot up. She turned and looked at Anna. "It's the only way! There's no other way to travel unless you are in that special state of mind!" Abby said to Anna. "You and I both know that." Abby playfully tossed her head again and took a few prancing steps. Abby kept her front legs placed firmly on the ground and her hind legs danced little steps in a semicircle in a hoppity hop kind of motion. She sure was playful and full of energy, Anna noticed.

"You know I'm ready to go, don't you Anna? I'm READY! Let's go meet her!" Abby said. "I see you have the packs ready. Let's GO! *LET'S GO!!!*"

Anna smiled. She hadn't seen this level of excitement in Abby since their days of running in arenas all over the Southwest region of the United States. They had been to the East Coast, and many times to Texas and Oklahoma, but mostly they were competing in the Southwest.

"You've been happy here, Abby, haven't you?" Anna asked carefully. She had been wanting to ask this question all these years but never really had the courage to ask it so directly. This was a totally different lifestyle for both of them. Anna had made her choice and with that choice, Abby's choice was made as well. "I could have sent you back on your own, you know," Anna said.

"Nope," Abby said, her mouth full of grass. "It only works with a horse *AND* her rider. Together. That means a pair who believes, who are in sync with one another. It doesn't work for one or the other to go alone," Abby continued. "You know how it works, Anna."

"But, my friend, you didn't answer my question," Anna continued. Anna took a look all around the valley. The grass was lush, the air light and cheerful. Wildflowers grew along the edges of the pasture. Beautiful wooden homes dotted the countryside. The spectacular mountains of the Alps rose in the background. The sun was on Abby's back warming her nicely as a cool but calm and gentle breeze flowed through the valley.

Anna had her medical practice and often traveled to other valleys to help the villagers who were sick or injured. Sometimes patients even traveled quite far to see her. But when Anna received an urgent call for help, usually by a banging at the door at night, Abby never hesitated to rise to the occasion to deliver Anna safely to a patient's home to administer care.

It had been the most painful decision of her life when Anna decided to stay. That was a long time ago and she was glad for her decision. But by making that decision, she had taken Abby from her herd too and even though they were a team, part of Anna knew she should have asked Abby more clearly if she wanted to stay here as well.

"Anna, you silly cowgirl, you know how happy I am. I'm with *YOU*. If I am with you I am happy anywhere. You should know that. You take care of me. We take care of one another. I am happy wherever you are. Besides," and with this, Abby pranced joyfully and made a few quick turns in the pasture, "look where I get to live!!!"

Anna laughed. She simply could not stop laughing. "All right, girl," she said. "I get it. We are a team. I'm happy here with you and you are with me so let's forget I asked, okay? Come on over here with me please and let's get tacked up. We have a journey to make. Let's go find that other Traveler!"

CHAPTER FOURTEEN

THE MOTHER HAS A QUESTION

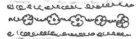 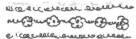

It was early the next morning and Liza was dressed. She had fed and watered Libby and the other animals and after a bit, had tacked up Libby and was preparing to go. The family had said their goodbyes and the children, though eager to stay and learn more about Liza, had already headed off for their chores. Liza noticed that the Father was near the stable making small repairs.

Liza packed the saddlebags with the gifts of food, a woolen blanket and warm clothing to wear in the cold mountains. With all the food she was given, Liza had the feeling the Mother wanted Liza to be prepared for a long journey.

The Mother stood nearby and was observing every move that Liza made. Liza was slightly uncomfortable only because she felt that she was going to be asked a question that she wasn't sure how to answer.

"Liza," the Mother said. "I think you know now that I know."

Liza turned to look at her. Liza had stiffened for a moment and then instantly relaxed when she saw the calm and kind look on the Mother's face.

"I think you know that I know you are a Traveler from another world." She paused after she said this. "That's what we call people like yourself. Travelers. You are the youngest one by the way."

Liza looked startled and the Mother continued.

"There are a few of you, actually. I have met one before, a very special and incredible woman. She came through here many years ago. When I saw you, I knew instantly that you were from another place, as she was."

Liza got a quizzical look in her eyes and immediately got concerned because now at that moment, she saw a pleading look in the woman's eyes. Liza was a little bit frightened.

"There are others?" Liza asked hesitantly.

"Yes," the Mother replied. "But I have only met just one." The Mother paused and before Liza could ask any questions, she continued.

"Liza, I don't want to know anything about your world or your place in time. I can see that we are similar and yet different. You have more modern things with you it seems, not dramatically more modern from what I can see, but even so, I know you are from another place in time that is advanced. But in light of this, I want to ask you a very important question. I want to ask you only one question actually. And I think you will be able to answer me and in doing so, I would like for you to be as honest with me as you can be. Please keep your answers very simple and very direct. Would you do that for me Liza?" Meia's mother asked.

"I will, ma'am," Liza said. Libby was standing nearby and stood very still and she was very quiet. She didn't stomp her feet and she didn't even swish her tail. Instead, Libby was focused and her ears moved with every movement the woman made and with every movement that Liza made. She was listening very intently.

"Liza, you know what year it is don't you?"

"Yes ma'am, I do. It's all quite unbelievable but I know it's all true now. I'm in the 1880's."

"Then all I want to know is if there is anything I need to do to protect my family." The Mother stated her words as calmly as she could.

Liza was shocked. This was not a question she was expecting. She was visibly taken aback and she looked quickly over at Libby. "I'm a child," she thought to herself. "An adult is asking me a very adultlike question and I think I know the answer she seeks, but I don't know what I'm supposed to do," she thought, desperately trying to decide how to best answer the question. Liza turned back to look at the Mother. Then Liza looked back over at Libby again and it was almost as though Libby had read her mind. Liza arched her eyebrows as she thought she heard a voice in her head. "It can't be," Liza said to herself.

"Tell her, Liza."

Liza almost jumped. "Did Libby say that out loud? Meia's Mother hasn't looked over at Libby. But I heard Libby speak. What just happened?" Liza asked herself.

"Tell her, Liza," Libby said again. And this time, Meia's mother glanced over at Libby, and then turned back to look at Liza again.

Liza got a very mature look on her face. "You have all been so friendly to me. I have learned so much and I have enjoyed your family and my time here very much," Liza said with solemn confidence.

She paused and took an intake of breath. She had to think carefully and speak precisely. She exhaled slowly.

"About thirty years from now, the world will go to war. And it will be awful. And it will be throughout Europe. Everywhere. It won't exactly come to Switzerland, but you will be affected, even here in the mountains somewhat," Liza said with measured accuracy.

At this, Meia's mother held her breath for a moment but said nothing. Libby nodded approvingly.

"Thank you," the woman said.

Then she did something quite unexpected. She looked down to her belly and stroked it.

With that very feminine movement of her hand on her belly, Liza's eyes shot wide open. Her eyes followed the movement of the woman's hand. It wasn't just a stroke; she was caressing her belly lovingly.

Then Meia's mother looked over at her daughter, hard at work in the garden, and up into the hills at her son, already hard at work with the animals while he led them to the grazing pastures. She looked at her husband, who was working near the woodpile.

She smiled as she stroked her belly again and she smiled as she looked over at her family. "We will prepare," the Mother said finally.

"Wait!" Liza said. Liza shook her head and looked down. This part was awful for her, but she continued.

"And it will happen again about twenty years after that. Both wars will last about five years. If you have family in other countries, try to get them to come here. When you begin to hear that awful things are happening, believe everything you hear and prepare as much as you can," Liza said. Liza looked at the Mother's belly. "Teach everyone to prepare," Liza continued.

Meia's mother was shocked at this second bit news, but remained silent and then she shook her head slightly.

"Well, I am not surprised," the Mother said. "Thank you, Liza. I don't want to know anything more. I have always believed that it is good to be prepared mentally, physically and financially and to have plenty of supplies. We have a strong family and we have many wise friends. We will live our lives with happiness and joy and we will prepare as well. I will prepare, that is. I will not tell anyone what I know because that will frighten them and they would not believe me anyway most likely. Only people who have met Travelers will understand and I will be discrete. When the time comes, I will tell a few who will understand me and who will believe me. Thank you, Liza. I know that must have been very difficult for you," she said finally.

Liza exhaled. She realized she had been holding her breath. This was difficult news to have delivered, but she was glad the woman understood and would prepare.

Then Liza smiled at her and said, "Once again, I would like to thank you for being so kind to me. You did not treat me as an outsider but welcomed me into your family. My horse Libby and I are grateful. But I want to add that good things are coming as well. Your children will know prosperity and all the good changes coming to this world will be good for them too!" Liza said. Liza was confused for a moment and thought, "How did I know that? How did I know to tell the Mother what I just said about her children?"

She waved that thought away in her mind. And with that, Liza gave the woman a hug and swung up into the saddle. "I'm only twelve years old. My mother always told me it's good to be a child but it's good to know adult things too. When she teaches me things about history and different countries, I always listen. And she always tells me the truth. That's why I told you the truth when you asked, even though it was a difficult truth," Liza said finally.

"Farewell my young friend, my young Traveler friend. Follow the signs. The gift my husband gave to you will serve as a guide. It is more than a gift, it is part of a map. Look for the signs. They will guide you," the Mother said earnestly.

Liza nodded. Then the Mother added, "I'm not sure you completely understood what I said earlier. It's that you are not the only Traveler! You will find others. You need to find the others."

Then the Mother looked at Libby. "Take good care of this young Traveler," she said to Libby.

"I will," said Libby.

Liza asked Libby to walk on with a squeeze of her legs into Libby's sides. But after only a few steps down the trail, Liza turned Libby suddenly and walked back to the Mother. She pulled a thick batch of note paper from her jacket pocket that was folded in quarters. As she looked at it, she nodded to herself. Liza returned back to the Mother and carefully held the papers out to her.

The Mother had a puzzled look on her face.

"Please take this," Liza urged. "Once you see what is written, promise me you will carefully use the information with wisdom and care. You will know what to do."

Opening one of the folded pages, the Mother quickly took a glance at some of what Liza had written on it - it was full of names, dates and historical comments. With a shocked look, the Mother lifted her head up and looked deeply and intently into Liza's eyes.

"So young and so wise," the Mother said. "On behalf of my family, I thank you. I will read this with great care and use the information wisely," she added. "Thank you again and goodbye my young friend. Be well."

And breathing a sigh of relief, Liza turned Libby and they headed off on the trail.

After a few moments of silence, Libby made a small nicker as though to clear her throat to speak.

"Liza?" Libby said.

"Yes, Libby," Liza replied.

"You did the right thing, Liza," Libby said after they got some distance between them and the chalet. "I know that was hard for you, Liza. When you told me that you were up half the night writing down every historical detail you could remember, I knew you would be torn whether or not to intervene. I get the feeling that Travelers aren't supposed to change anything they encounter here. But these people will need that information in the coming years. I am certain they will use what they've read wisely."

Then Libby paused. "Liza, you can't change the past, you know."

"I know," Liza said sadly. "But I had a feeling she might ask me some questions. I wasn't certain I would tell her anything. I'm glad I did and I'm glad I gave her my notes."

"You are quite the young lady, Liza, and I'm proud to be your friend," Libby said.

Liza stroked and patted Libby's neck and then asked her mare to pick up a light and easy trot.

CHAPTER FIFTEEN

ANNA HELPS A FAMILY

"What seems to be the trouble?" Anna asked, dropping down from Abby's back.

Anna absentmindedly but purposefully removed the bridle from Abby and then hung it over the saddle horn. She nimbly loosened the cinch two holes and then gave a quick reassuring pat on Abby's neck.

A worried man had run down the path from his home to the main path on which Anna and Abby had been traveling. Anna immediately saw he was distressed and pausing Abby, she had hopped off.

Anna already had a medium-sized leather pouch slung over her shoulder as she walked up the path to the house with the man. She had also grabbed her attending coat and apron that she wore for medical cases. Anna took a polite stretch just a bit to remove the stiffness that had crept up after several days in the saddle with Abby. "I'm not twenty-five anymore," she sighed quietly.

"We had gotten word you might be coming this way," the man said breathlessly. "One of us has been waiting by the window for two days," he explained. "Watching for you," he added, nervously looking back to Anna's horse, which he noticed had now been completely ignored by Anna. Then he looked over at Anna who didn't seem bothered.

Abby had slowly stepped away from Anna and the man and had found a patch of grass to eat. Abby was polite about it. Whenever Anna and Abby visited friends, or treated patients, or traveled for business in the valley, Abby always kept off their gardens and flowerbeds. She only ate the grasses that had grown too tall that someone had forgotten to trim. Abby seemed to take a special kind of pride in helping families tidy up their grassy spaces near their home. "I can be useful too," said Abby to herself, as she nibbled down a row of grasses near the garden fence that the scythe had missed.

Anna looked over at Abby and sighed, "There she goes again. I hope I don't have to explain why I don't put a halter on my horse and how I absolutely know my horse won't run off," Anna thought. "Oh boy. At least she's mowing the grass again!" Anna shook her head and smiled a little then immediately put on her professional demeanor once more.

Turning back to the man, Anna motioned the man forward then picked up her pace and marched into the house after him. "Right then," Anna said. "Let's look at the patient."

However, just before they entered the home, Anna noticed that the man had made one more glance back at Abby. She saw that Abby had looked up and was watching the two of them in the doorway. At that moment, Abby made a calm easy snort and blew and shook her head just a bit. Anna saw the man's face relax. Often times, Anna noticed it was just like that. Patients or their families usually calmed down whenever they saw Abby.

After a few hours, Anna emerged with a grateful family surrounding her. "Oh, thank you, Miss Anna, thank you," they chorused. "We are so glad you came. We are so grateful to you!" they echoed again.

Anna held up a hand with her palm pressed into the air in a show of honest but firm modesty, and she thanked the family right back. She was grateful that this was a simple medical case for her to manage and not something requiring surgery or assistance from another doctor. Usually, she found that relieving pressure on a wound using heat or ice worked wonders. Likewise cleansing a festering wound more thoroughly or making a quick stitch or two on a deep cut seemed to take care of most problems when her patients needed medical attention. Other times, special herbal teas or salves were required. Anna always had her leather medical pouch with her, even if she only went a few miles from her chalet.

Several years ago, one quick trip down the valley to see a friend had turned into several days of medical visits further down the valley and up into the foothills of the mountains. As a result, Anna learned that whenever she went out on horseback with Abby, she also packed extra clothing and extra supplies, just in case.

Anna was glad for the broad range of medicine she had learned and practiced, and for all of her surgical experience. She found that all of this knowledge helped her here in this world everywhere she went. She enjoyed the challenges of the more complicated cases especially well and had developed a network of colleagues throughout the Alps and further away. Often times, it seemed her colleagues asked for her advice more than she found it necessary to ask for theirs. They didn't seem to mind and she didn't either. "Nothing better than brainstorming on a medical case," Anna recalled.

As she turned to leave, she saw Abby there in the grass, lying down flat out. Her legs were stiff and straight and almost looked like she had, well, like she had died. Anna could see that Abby was breathing.

"That funny horse of mine has fallen asleep again," Anna said out loud. "Too much energy, then *BAM*. Zonked out," she said and then laughed.

"Okay Abby, get up my friend, get up!" Anna laughed, as she gave her horse a playful poke on the butt and then a firm but friendly swat to hurry Abby's movements along.

"Yes, ma'am, I'm up, I'm up," Abby cried, climbing to her feet. Her front legs stuck out in front of her and pressed into the ground, then Abby pulled herself up onto her back legs. She leaned forward and shook and all the leather straps and flaps and pouches and possessions made funny flapping noises as she shook. They both laughed.

"Wait, shhhhhh, don't say anything more," Anna said. "They don't know about us and the family is watching," Anna said in a quiet voice and making another, "shhhhhh," sound.

Abby laughed.

"Seriously, don't you dare, you silly mare," Anna said as she stepped forward and rubbed Abby on the forehead and patted her neck.

"We need to keep going," Anna said. "I get the feeling that we will be on the trails into the mountains for a few more days until we find the Traveler," Anna stressed.

"Right you are, Anna. I'm ready! Fed, rested and ready," Abby exclaimed.

Putting the bridle back on Abby and fastening her medical pouch to the saddle and tightening up the cinch, Anna checked the saddle and the saddlebags. Then she stepped up into the stirrup and swung up onto the saddle. She got her other foot into the second stirrup and stood up for a moment and then sat down to get her seat properly set for another many miles on the trails with Abby.

With a professional nod of her head back to the family, Anna asked Abby for a walk, and then asked for a fast trot and they both moved off. Abby was anxious to get going after her little nap, so she picked up the pace right away.

"Let's head on up North for a long while girl," Anna said. "I want to beat this rain that might be coming in. You feel it in the air too, right, girl?" Anna asked.

"Yes, I do, Anna. And a storm in the Alps isn't any fun at all," Abby said, shaking her head like she was shaking a memory out from the past.

Anna thought back to the time they were in a chalet on a mountainside in a vicious storm. They were helping a woman deliver a baby that was breech, and the weather outside was horrendous. Although Abby had figured out how to settle herself into the stable without any help, Anna was inside the chalet with a very nervous first-time mother and father with no help available to calm either of them.

Abby always seemed to know when to fix up her own situation for the night by herself. She would nudge Anna to remove the saddle altogether right away or at least to loosen her cinch and remove her bridle. Then Abby would stroll off and mow the grass for the chalet owner and find a place to stay for the night if she realized Anna would be busy for a while with patients. Sometimes people noticed the loyal independence of Anna's horse, and once someone tried to catch Abby and tie her up for Anna. But Anna would always say, "Abby won't go anywhere. Leave her be. She's fine."

That night was a massive storm for the history books however. The rain was thick and heavy and the lightening was striking everywhere. Rain was falling sideways it seemed and it was a violent storm for sure. Trees were falling and it felt like parts of the mountain were sliding down from all the rain. Abby remembered that even though she felt safe in the stable, she was worried for Anna inside the chalet.

Anna had thought about Abby outside in the storm as well, and had to hope for the best while she was inside with scared parents-to-be. A few times, when trees fell, Anna looked out the window toward the stable and tried not to worry. Once, however, she caught sight of Abby peaking her head out and looking for Anna there in the chalet! "What a loyal friend she is," Anna remembered thinking.

The storm had subsided finally and that morning, over the crunching and munching of her hay, Abby heard the cry of a newborn baby. "So, the night had ended well," Abby recalled, thinking back on it all. And at that precise moment, Abby knew that nothing could ever stop Anna from taking care of important medical work, not even a massive Alpine lightning and thunderstorm.

So today, after helping yet another family, they were back on the trails. Anna made a click to send Abby up into an even faster trot and then kissed her up into a slow lope, and they headed up into the mountains. Off in the distance if anyone was listening, they would have heard two voices talking away.

Anna and Abby followed trails that split off from the main road-like trail into smaller trails that went deeper into the mountains. They went over tree roots and large patches of moss and over long stretches of soft pine needle trails as they made their way ever closer to the Traveler.

Anna felt they were getting closer. Abby did too. Every now and then Abby would ask Anna to stop and then Abby would throw her head into the air and whinny. Then she would sniff the air and blow, usually a hard blow through her nostrils. After a few moments, Abby would pick up a trot or a lope once again and they would continue on.

They found a nice quiet place along a mountain stream to stop for the night. After settling down, Anna pulled out some food she had prepared and the few items of food given as a thank you gift from the family she had just helped. The cheese was delicious and Anna treated herself to several of their baked sweets.

"I'm excited to meet a new Traveler, Anna," Abby said.

"I am too, Abby," Anna replied.

"I hope her horse is nice," said Abby.

Anna smiled. "I'm sure she is," she said to Abby.

There was a special kind of calm energy in the air as they prepared to bed down for the night. The rain Anna thought might be coming was just a cold front that came in, and she was glad for her warm bedroll. In the Alps, you always had to pack for three seasons, it seemed, because the weather was so variable.

Anna organized the saddle and other tack she had taken off Abby and made a mental note of the items she would need to obtain to refresh her supplies in her leather medical pouch. In the meantime, Abby dropped her nose to the ground and bumped the grasses down with occasional stomping of her hooves as if to flatten everything out. She had already eaten her fill and once she had nosed everything into place and stomped around, Abby did a little circle and then dropped down to the ground, knees first, the way horses do that want to sleep.

That night, instead of grazing during the night, Abby chose to lie down into a kind of cat-like, almost sphinxlike pose; alert but restful. She waited for Anna to nestle on the ground up against her.

"I like lying here next to you, Abby," Anna said.

"I like having you next to me too, Anna," Abby said.

Their mutual warmth was soothing to the other. And pretty soon, they both went to sleep.

CHAPTER SIXTEEN

SOMETHING HURTS

Liza and Libby had been on the mountain trails for many days. Although Liza kept her eye out, she didn't see any of the signs except once. They went past a chalet that had the sign of the Traveler carved into a wooden part of the wall just below the roofline. As they got closer to the chalet, they saw that it was closed up without anyone at home. It was inhabited but it seemed to look as though everyone who lived there was simply gone for the day.

"Should we stay and wait for them to come home, Libby-girl?" Liza had asked.

Libby pondered for a moment and then said, "But what if they are out visiting family, or doing business in another village, or are up with their herds in the mountains somewhere, Liza. We might be waiting for days," Libby said thoughtfully. "It sure would be nice to meet these people since they were dedicated enough to carve the sign into the side of their chalet. But I think we should keep pressing on," she continued.

"I agree, girl," Liza had said regrettably. "It sure would have been nice to have met those people," Liza thought. "But Libby you are right. We should press on."

After days and days of travel in the mountains, they had encountered their share of varying temperatures. On some days there in the mountains, like Anna, they experienced three different levels of weather. There were days of a wet chilly mist, afternoons of bright sunshine, and evenings that were cool and brisk. Liza kept her jackets handy, tied with the leather straps on the back of her saddle, and she would start the day with one jacket, remove it and change to another one, and then later in the day, not be wearing a jacket at all, it seemed. But today in particular was simply a beautiful day for riding. Not only was the weather spectacular but the views were as well.

Everywhere Liza looked, she saw lush small pastures tucked within steep hillsides and along rolling areas of the mountainsides. She was stunned at how steeply the pastures rose up into the mountains and yet sheep and cows wandered all over and up and down like it wasn't even a challenge for them.

Every now and then she saw herders tending their flocks. Some stood up to wave and Liza cheerfully waved back. There were all kinds of colorful flowers blooming in the pastures. The scenery was spectacular. There were steep, jagged, snowcapped mountains everywhere and it seemed that each one was lovelier than the next. Now that Liza knew she was in the Swiss Alps, and she knew what time period it was, she tried very hard to remember her geography lessons as well as her history lessons.

Sometimes, subconsciously, she would frown a moment as she thought about the geology of how these amazing mountains were formed, and then she would get a knowing 'aha' moment when she remembered what she had been taught about both geography and geology.

Her mother had once been keenly interested in going out and collecting fossils and different kinds of rocks, and over time and throughout their travels, had accumulated quite a nice little collection. Her mother kept these collections on display in a hobby room of her own at their house back on the East Coast. Thinking about her studies and her parents made her happy, though wistful at times. But then her face would relax into a smile. "Libby told me to enjoy the experiences I would have," Liza recalled and resolved to keep going on.

One of the things Liza and Libby had been enjoying was loping at different speeds along the trails. Both of them were exhilarated by the feeling of the wind against their faces and they were excited by the energy they both felt running hard and fast.

"Run, Libby, run!" Liza would say.

"Let go of the reins, Liza," Libby said one time and as they ran, Liza lifted her arms out to the side and looked up into the heavens. Liza knew that Libby felt wild and free at times like these, and so she let her run as fast as she wanted to run. It was all such a good feeling for both of them.

On this day, as the afternoon wore on, they had been trotting along the trails with some occasional walking. Libby hadn't really gotten up too much of a sweat in the early part of the day, but the sun had come up and although the air was cool and clean and fresh, Libby was wet now, what with all the active walking, trotting and loping.

Liza leaned forward and patted the side of Libby's neck. She left her hand there for a moment and could feel Libby's damp warmth.

A few moments earlier, there had been a chance for Libby to enjoy a drink of a mountain stream. They had been ambling along quietly in the last hour and Liza brought them from their trot down to a calm halt with her gentle, "Whoa," and a nice sit-down movement into the saddle. Lately, Liza had barely used her reins to guide her mare. Libby knew what to do now, more so than ever.

After they came to a stop, Liza dismounted and removed Libby's bridle and reins and hung them from her saddle horn. Libby walked to the stream to drink but only after first dropping her head and yanking out some lush grass to eat. Liza stood with the sun on her face as Libby chomped away, and watched as Libby walked over to the stream. When Libby came back, she dropped her head again and began to eat some more grass.

While she stood there beside Libby, Liza took the opportunity to gather up some food for herself. She searched around in her pack that was secured to Libby's saddle. She removed some food items from it and stuffed them into her pockets. Then she walked over to the stream and got down on her hands and knees and took a good long drink from the stream.

"Aaaaah," Liza said and giggled to herself when she stood back up. She took a little stretch, which felt good after all the riding.

After they had gotten going again, Liza wasn't certain but thought she noticed a slight change in Libby's gait. Libby didn't say anything and Liza soon forgot about it as she pulled some food out of her pocket. She still had some snack food from Arizona even after these many days on the trails, but her packs were also full with foods from her visit with Meia's family,

"This is all very tasty," Liza said. "I pulled out some cheese and some bread and some dried meat and I've been snacking, Libby. I don't think I've ever had anything so fresh and wonderful," she continued. Liza was a little lost in her thoughts as she enjoyed the fresh food and remembered how tasty and refreshing the water was from the mountain stream.

Libby slowed down a bit and after a few moments, Liza noticed Libby's gait once again. Something did not feel right.

"Uh, Libby, hey girl, are you okay?" Liza asked.

Libby remained silent for a few more steps.

"Libby-girl, are you alright?"

Liza asked Libby to stop, shoved the snacks back into her pockets and then immediately jumped off Libby.

Liza walked to stand in front of Libby. "Hey, girl, what's up?" Liza asked again.

Libby looked into the distance off to one side. Then she turned her head and looked at Liza and did a gentle snort and blow through her nose. It always sounded like Libby was going to make some kind of important pronouncement after she took a deep inhale and then made a loud exhale like that.

"Well," said Libby, "well, well, well, well, well," she continued, almost as though she was frustrated with herself.

"And?" said Liza.

"I should have said something sooner. But to be honest, in the past, you would have noticed something sooner if we had been back in Arizona or anywhere out on a trail ride," Libby said, turning away a little bit.

Liza got concerned. "Libby, what's wrong?" Suddenly Liza stepped back and took a look at Libby and how she was standing. Liza gazed all over Libby's body. She analyzed the look of each leg and gently picked up each hoof to examine the shoe and the frog and then ran her hands over each leg to examine for any heat. Liza stood up again and stepped back.

Then she saw it. It was clear as day.

Libby's hind left leg was ever so slightly elevated even though she was clearly still weight-bearing. It was hard to see but there was definitely something wrong.

Liza didn't panic. She knew what to do. She gently returned to that leg and bent over and lifted Libby's leg up and Liza examined the shoe and the frog and everything else once again.

"I wish I had some hoof testers with me but we never carry those in the equine first aid kit," Liza muttered.

"Liza, I can tell you what is wrong. I think I have a stone bruise," Libby said quietly. "I'm okay to continue but I might be better off if we took a break for a day perhaps," Libby sighed.

Liza jumped into action. "I'm so sorry, girl. I should have been more aware. I was looking all around and enjoying the scenery. I was lost in my thoughts. But also, I've become so used to you just telling me things, that I forgot that it's my job to feel your gait as we walk and trot and lope, and for me to notice *EVERYTHING* about you."

"I'm sorry too," Libby said. "I keep forgetting that we are in another world now and even though everything is new to us and we have different scenery and experiences happening to us, I simply forgot to *SAY SOMETHING*," Libby said.

Liza threw her arms around Libby's neck then pulled back and stroked her and patted her.

"I know what to do, girl. It's no one's fault. We are both learning how to communicate with one another here now and I should have been more aware, regardless. Let's get this saddle off of you and get you into the cold water to stand and cool off that hoof for you. I'm pretty sure I felt some heat there."

Libby closed her eyes and looked calm and happy.

Taking the reins, Liza walked Libby over to a small mountain hut that she had noticed just ahead on the trail. It seemed in good shape but it looked completely deserted for this time of year. There were many reasons why mountain huts might be deserted and Liza wondered if anyone would mind if they used the hut for a night or two.

Liza took her time to carefully remove all the tack and set it on the ground. Normally, in their world, she would be putting a halter on Libby to lead her wherever they needed to go. Back home, sometimes, Liza would simply toss the lead rope over Libby's neck and they would walk side by side. There, Liza felt she needed to lead Libby.

Here, in this world, the halter wasn't necessary at all. Libby would just walk right beside Liza without having to be led. And Liza could tell Libby where they were going or could tell her to walk over here or walk over there.

Actually, Liza had begun to wonder if Libby would ever need a halter again now that they experienced this kind of trust between them. "So why ever use the halter?" Liza asked herself as she walked with Libby.

But for sure, right now it absolutely wasn't needed, so Liza did not untie it from the back of her saddle.

"Let's get you over to the stream, girl," Liza said.

The trail they had been on meandered along a stream and fortunately, the hut was nearby. After removing Libby's tack over at the hut, they walked back to the stream and searched for a spot that seemed as smooth as possible.

"Oh, wow this feels great," Libby said once she walked all the way into the water.

Libby stood there in the stream and seemed relaxed. Liza looked at her watch and said, "Twenty minutes girl! You know the drill! Any injury always seems to need twenty minutes of cold hosing back home, so let's have you stand in the stream for twenty minutes. Then we will do it again in a bit." Libby gave a small nicker of delight.

"I've been kind of carefully picking my way along the trails but I must have stepped on a sharp rock or something a while back when we were loping," Libby said. "I've been looking at the scenery too, you know, so I missed something and stepped incorrectly."

"That's okay, girl," Liza said. "We aren't in a hurry. This is a pretty spot and we have the mountain hut we can use, so let's do everything right and get you all fixed up," Liza continued.

Libby thought for a moment and said, "Liza, you know I've never been able to really thank you for all the ways you take care of me. It's so much nicer being your horse than I imagine it would be as a wild horse out in the open."

Liza stood and looked at Libby.

Libby continued, "Anytime something has been wrong or if I've had a cut or a bruise or anything, I want you to know how wonderful you have been to me. I remember the time my front leg was injured and you were all bent over with the hose near my lower leg for twenty long minutes. You stood there so diligently and you leaned into me and I leaned into you the whole time. I remember it was a very cold day and I knew you were cold and uncomfortable but you stood there and took good care of me," Libby said. "And you did it day after day and never complained."

Liza kept looking at Libby. Libby paused.

"Sometimes that water would be really cold. But I always stood there pretty nicely for you because there was something about how calm you were with me and how caring your voice was. Well, when you take care of me like that, I know what you are doing. I try my best to be good and to stand still whenever you are taking care of me," Libby said. "Sometimes I'm not very patient, and I'm sorry for the times I wouldn't stand quietly," she continued. "I know I can be really difficult sometimes," Libby added, somewhat sheepishly.

Liza felt her eyes getting watery. She kept looking at Libby.

"Well," Libby continued, "I think I need to really apologize for sometimes being a little impatient and even kind of antsy at the end of twenty minutes of cold hosing, and sometimes not always standing still for you. I guess I always knew you were doing good things for me but now that we can actually tell one another what we think, well, I want you to know how much I appreciate how you take care of me."

Liza stood quietly and just let the tears flow down her face. She still could not believe that she and Libby could talk to one another and have full conversations in a language they both understood. Everything here was so clear to both of them and it was all so special. So these were happy tears and Libby understood that too.

"Aw, that's okay girl. I love you, you know!"

"I love you too, Liza."

And for just a while longer they stood there together, with Libby in the mountain stream, and Liza on the bank, with her hand on Libby's withers, calmly petting her.

CHAPTER SEVENTEEN

THE MOUNTAIN HUT

It wasn't hard for Liza to have noticed that little mountain hut which was situated off the trail on the edge of a grassy meadow. Liza knew that farmers and shepherds used every moment of sunshine and access to abundant grasses to feed their herds of cows and sheep. The summers were short up here in the Alps and she knew shepherds brought their herds up into the mountains and usually lived with them, even for the entire summer. The huts offered shelter from summer storms and gave the shepherds a place to live temporarily.

"It's unusual for a hut and a meadow full of grass like this to go unused at this time of year," Liza said to Libby. Liza had started to walk back to the hut and Libby slowly strolled along beside her. As Liza looked the hut over, Libby took a few steps past Liza.

"Ooooh, lovely grass," Libby said.

Libby dropped her head and started munching away. When she lifted her head to look at Liza, some long grasses were hanging from her mouth.

"You look positively silly, Libby!" Liza exclaimed.

It's quite possible Libby lifted an eye muscle a bit, somewhat in mock horror but more in a teasing manner.

Liza giggled.

"As I was saying, I wonder why no one is here?" asked Liza, with a pensive look on her face.

When Libby had finished chewing, she said, "Maybe there was an illness or a death in the shepherd's family and no one can get the herd up here," she said with a wizened note to her voice. "Or sometimes an entire herd can get an illness and then the shepherd has to take time to build up a herd again," Libby continued.

The hut looked very well-maintained. That much was evident from the perfect slate roof and all the tightly chinked logs of the walls of the hut. The door looked sound. The window shutters were unbroken and the frames looked well-made. There was a little path to the doorway and although no flowers were in the window boxes, some wildflowers had evidently seeded themselves. Pretty blue delicate flowers had popped up in the two neatly made window boxes hanging under the windows located on either side of the door.

"Girl, I think you are correct," Liza said.

Then Libby noticed that Liza had a frown on her face.

"Liza?" Libby asked.

"Yep," she replied.

"Liza, what are you thinking?"

"Well, I'm wondering what to do actually. You are injured and fortunately right here in our travels, there is a lovely safe place to stay. Do you think it would be okay to use this hut for a few nights while we rest and you recover?" Liza asked hesitantly.

Libby kept looking at the hut and Liza could see that she was thinking.

Liza waited.

"Here's what I think," Libby said. "You are careful and considerate. And you are respectful of personal property. I see that in the way you take care of me, of my tack and of your own possessions. I notice things like that you know," Libby said.

Liza's face was pensive.

"What's more, it's my guess that there are unwritten rules up here in the mountains," Libby continued.

"What do you mean?" asked Liza.

"I mean that people should not take or use what is not theirs. Even way up here, where no one is looking. But if they are in trouble, as we are, as long as they respect another's property, here in the mountains, far from help, I think it's all okay," said Libby.

"So," Liza paused, "then what you are saying is..."

"Yes, Liza," Libby interrupted, "it's okay to spend the night here and to use the hut," she said. "But we both must respect everything and leave it in better condition than we found it. Agreed?"

After clapping her hands together and giving a nod, Liza walked to the entrance of the hut to explore. She saw carefully placed stones on either side of the path. She noticed that the roofline was very steep, probably to increase the strength of the roof when there were heavy snows. Liza imagined that up here, there was probably lots and lots of snow and that a roof like this most likely had to carry tons of weight for months at a time.

She carefully examined the metal latch on the heavy wooden door. She could see that the door was well-made and she observed that it had carved designs in it. "Someone has taken a lot of pride in this mountain hut," Liza thought to herself. She also noticed that the heavy wooden shutters had designs carved and cut into them. They looked secured from the inside.

Liza hesitated, looked at the door again, took a deep breath, and pressed on the metal latch pin. The door opened! It was not locked! That seemed to prove Libby's theory that when in danger, mountain huts might be used by others.

When she opened the door, Liza hung back for a moment just to make sure nothing flew up into her face from the inside of the hut, and that nothing ran out the door either. Sometimes insects, birds, varmints or even larger animals found their way into cabins back home and she didn't want anything flying or running to come out and run smack into her! Fortunately, nothing did. Liza knew that meant this hut was even more well-made than she had initially thought.

It was still daylight, so Liza could see inside clearly enough. She walked to one of the windows and opened it a bit and unlatched the shutters. She secured the shutters open and kept the window open as well for fresh air. Then she turned to do the same to the other window and shutters.

As she looked around inside, Liza was stunned at what she saw once the sunlight came into the hut.

This was a woodcarver's paradise! Clearly it was the hut of a shepherd but there was a large carpenter's bench with more than a dozen chisels of various shapes and sizes hanging in front of it. Roughly milled pieces of wood and thick chunky blocks of wood in all sizes, perfect for carving, lay beside the bench. All around the bench on the walls were shelves full of dozens of wooden figurines. There were animals, people, trees, small buildings, flowers and more. The details were outstanding. In fact, they were incredible. Liza could see that a real professional made quite the summer home here.

Liza looked around her and saw that in one corner of the hut there was a kind of wardrobe that was open-faced. Liza saw men's clothing hanging there. Pants, jackets, long-sleeved shirts and several hats were all hanging from wooden pegs. Socks and other clothing lay folded on a shelf. Several types of boots were arranged on the floor in a row.

One wall of the hut had the tools of a shepherd. It seems this hut was used both to live in and to store supplies. There were leather and wooden yolks with large bells for cows hanging from several wooden hooks. There was a large scythe for slashing through the lush mountain grasses hanging next to some tools for cutting and splitting wood.

There was a small woodstove for cooking and for warmth, and along another wall, some wood was stacked. Liza had seen lots of stacked wood outside as well. Beside the stove were shelves of some kitchen items with a few plates, silverware and sturdy mugs. On top of the stove was a large pot with a lid for cooking. Ladles and stirring utensils as well as cutting knives hung from pegs.

The floors were made of heavy planks of wood pegged to supporting logs underneath. The floor was all straight and true. A large, handmade, thick, colorful woolen carpet filled the middle of the room.

One bed was in the far corner. Liza opened a trunk at the foot of the bed and was astonished. She found sheets, pillows, towels and a puffy down comforter.

Everything was clean, almost as though the shepherd had finished the summer, gone down below into the valley to his home and brought back fresh supplies for the following year. All neat as a pin!

Liza ran to the door.

"Libby, we are all set here," she cried.

Libby walked over to the hut and up the path to the front door. Liza saw a slight limp and was instantly relieved that she had decided to rest with her.

Libby poked her head in the door and nodded her head in approval. Liza walked over to Libby and rubbed her cheek and neck.

"Girl, let's get your hoof to soaking in the stream once again and I'll get a bucket of water for me for drinking," Liza said.

However, before she searched for a bucket, Liza paused for one moment and looked thoughtful. Then she turned around and walked to the back wall of the hut. There was a small door there.

"I wonder," Liza said.

She opened it.

It led into a covered area that looked like it would be good for Libby. The roofline of the hut extended out over this area, almost cantilever style, with several strong supporting beams and rough walls on either side. This would make a nice enclosure for Libby for sure.

Liza started to run back to the front door but looked around and saw that Libby had discovered this back portion of the hut. She was already peaking her head inside and was looking at Liza. She stood there looking kind of goofy, Liza decided, as she peaked in like that. Liza just smiled at her goofy horse.

"Well now!" Libby exclaimed. "You know I will be happy outside in the meadow all by myself but it will be nice to have a way to come under this roofline and be closer to you, Liza!" Libby said.

Liza threw her arms around Libby's neck again and hugged her. "I know!" she said.

"Let's get your tack stored back here in this area," Liza added.

After carrying the tack through the little hut to the back, Liza laid everything inside this covered area. As she started to untie the halter from the loops on the side of the saddle, Liza said, "Well I think we agreed that I don't need a halter with you anymore, do I girl."

Libby said, "Nope."

Liza grabbed a bucket from inside the hut, and together, they walked side by side to the stream. Liza filled the water bucket and put it on the bank of the steam. Libby stepped into the water and turned to stand close by Liza. She dropped her head to have a drink and when she lifted her head, she looked at Liza, looked at the mountain view, and then stood quietly.

Liza carefully slid her hand up to Libby's neck and under Libby's mane. It was warm there. She rubbed on Libby and stroked her hand down her neck to Libby's withers. Then she rubbed on Libby's back where the saddle had been and used two hands to make a currying motion all over Libby's back and then down underneath her belly. Liza rubbed her hands in a massaging motion all over Libby and made gentle scratches.

"That feels wonderful," Libby said as she leaned into Libby's hands for a deeper rub.

"Let me take a look at your hoof again, girl," Liza said. She pulled a hoof pick out of her back pocket. She had grabbed it from her pack before they left the hut. Liza bent over and gently leaned into Libby's leg as a cue for her to pick up her hoof. As usual, Libby lifted her leg up nicely for Liza as she carefully cleaned out the few bits of mud and grit that the water had not washed away.

Then Liza pressed on the sole with the edge of the hoof pick. She didn't have any hoof testers with her so this would have to do. She poked and prodded and Liza was looking for a reaction from Libby.

Still bent over, Liza said, "Well girl, this is silly. Here I am all bent over, examining you and looking to see if you are sensitive to this and that. All I have to do is ask you now, right?" Liza paused after she asked her question.

"I know you said you have a stone bruise. I just wanted to find out where, exactly," Liza explained.

Libby was quiet for a moment, lost in thought. Then she lifted her head up suddenly. She whinnied a bit up into the air. It was a quiet whinny but a long one.

"What's up, girl?" Liza asked. She stood up and took a step back and looked straight into Libby's face. "Did I do something wrong?"

There was a moment's pause.

"Liza, Liza, Liza, Liza," Libby said. "You said all you have to do now is just ask me questions about this or that. You're hinting that all you have to do is tell me to go do this or do that to take care of myself. I think that's obvious. Of course! I can walk over to the stream by myself. I can delicately step my own hoof into hard stones or onto a small rock to act like a hoof tester to see if my hoof is tender, and I can even do so much more for myself. I can tell you things and I can even boss you around as you use the bit and the reins and your spurs and legs on me," she continued. "I can tell you every single thing you might want to know about me. For sure." Libby paused after this little speech.

Liza got a pensive look on her face.

"Liza, my dear cowgirl, would you want that?" Libby asked.

Libby paused. Liza scrunched her face then looked pensive again.

"Would you want for me to be so independent that I don't really need you? Is that what you want?" Libby asked again. "Is that what you think I want?" Libby asked with a stronger but gentle question in her voice.

Liza looked at Libby and was puzzled.

"Liza, my dear cowgirl, you need to keep your skills intact. Sometimes you miss a cue, and sometimes you misinterpret me, but you almost always get it right with me. You know my moods. You know how I walk and how my body feels and its rhythm when we are walking, trotting, loping or galloping. You know how I should look weight wise and you know how I should feel. You take care of my feeding and care and veterinary concerns. You have my teeth floated and take excellent care of my hooves. You interpret what you see and feel every day. What if I tell you what you need to know all the time? Won't that hurt your skills? Won't that lessen your ability to understand me?" Libby asked.

Liza opened her mouth as if to say something, then closed it and remained quiet.

Then she spoke, thoughtfully and with a tinge of sadness.

"Libby, we aren't going to stay here forever are we," Liza stated both as a question and as a statement of fact. Liza got a small tear in her eye as a surge of emotions came over her. Libby was quiet and still. Liza stood closer to Libby and hung her arm over her mare's neck again.

"Liza, my dear, we are going to enjoy every moment that we can together as we speak to one another using your language," Libby said. "And we are going to learn things from one another each day that we are here," Libby continued. "And I will ask you questions and you will ask me questions. And we will talk and have good fun. But you must know that just as we got into this world by accident, there will be an opportunity to go back to our own world, whether by accident or by choice, and we will need to go, Liza," Libby continued once again.

Liza looked at Libby and looked deeply into her soft brown eyes. She saw the swirls of white hair on Libby's forehead. A vein pulsed on her big soft cheek. And Liza noticed Libby's incredibly long eyelashes. Liza stroked Libby's neck and back in beautiful, tender, long caresses.

"Libby, I'm enjoying talking to you and completely understanding you because you speak to me," Liza said. "I really, really like this," Liza continued. "I mean it. This is wonderful and it's a dream come true. I don't want it to end, girl, I don't," Liza said emphatically. "I don't want any of this to end," she cried, emotions flooding over her. Her voice had become passionate with the realization of what all of this meant.

Libby looked at Liza and leaned her head into Liza and nuzzled her and stayed right there next to Liza, keeping her warm and comforted.

"Liza, it doesn't matter which world we are in, I will always understand you. And you will always understand me. Words or not," Libby said gently.

Liza stood there as the sun began to go down and tears were flowing down her cheeks as she realized the truth in every single word Libby had just said.

"It's gonna be okay," Liza said to herself. "Everything I am experiencing is wonderful and will be good for me and good for my relationship with my horse. I am not going to be sad anymore. I am going to enjoy every moment I can!"

And then Liza smiled. She knew that the next few days would be good days to rest, reflect and recuperate. They had a safe place to stay with a solid roof for both of them. She had plenty of food and Libby had plenty of meadow grass. Liza already made plans to keep the hut tidy and to carefully clean up after Libby. Perhaps this mountain hut was a good place to settle down for these next few days after all.

Thinking about all of this, she knew that her time here at the hut with Libby would be excellent, and she already planned the thank-you note she would leave for the owner of this lovely mountain hut.

CHAPTER EIGHTEEN

ANNA FINDS LIZA

"Abby, you are just too full of energy!" Anna exclaimed.

Although Anna had relaxed her hands on the reins, occasionally she had to check Abby a tiny bit or else Abby would have been tearing across the countryside. It was in her genes. Abby was from terrific bloodlines and had the energy and running skills to match. With her magnificent quarter horse and thoroughbred lineage, this mare was built to run and she knew it!

Anna had actually chosen Abby due to her excellent mare lineage and that had paid off not just in her performance in the arenas, but in her intelligence and loyalty too.

"Aw, let's go, Anna," Abby exclaimed. "Just let up on the reins even more and let me run," Abby pleaded.

Anna smiled and laughed out loud. This wasn't the first time Abby had asked to just run, run, run.

"You are silly, my friend," Anna said. "Remember all the great fun we had barrel racing? Turning and burning and running free all over the Southwest? In arena after arena? I let you run then," Anna said laughing just a bit harder this time. "Remember?"

Abby was quiet. She had an idea what Anna was going to say next.

"But now we are a respectable pair, we are, and we need to present ourselves with elegance and grace as we travel," Anna said. "You never know when we might come across a village that needs us and if you've been running like crazy, some of my supplies might come flying out of the saddle bags just like the last time, remember?" Anna asked.

"When I jumped over that log, right? Is that what you mean?" said Abby. She sulked for a moment. Anna felt Abby's gait change to a calmer one, and felt as Abby relaxed all of her movements. "Okay fine, respectable it is," Abby said.

Abby took on a guilty look as she recalled the mess she had made of all of Anna's supplies while galloping like a wild thing and showing off.

Abby stopped prancing and Anna instantly relaxed her hands on the reins even more.

After a short while, they came across a wide-open meadow. Then Anna looked off onto the horizon up the trail through the meadow. She thought she saw something. The sun was in her eyes and she wasn't certain. But in an instant, she felt a warmth flood through her body.

"Oh my gosh," Anna said.

Anna looked again. Squinting, she could see a small rider on horseback.

Anna got a huge smile on her face and said, "Abby, we did it! We have found them! We did it, Abby! I just know that is the other Traveler! You feel it too, right?" Anna exclaimed.

"Yes!" said Abby. "I see them! I see them!" she cried.

Abby whinnied loudly and looked ahead at the horse and rider off in the distance. Then she whinnied again and again, crying out to the other horse. She was very noisy about it and full of energy. Her whinnies were almost ear splitting in how loud they were. She began to dance in place again. Anna had never seen Abby this excited in all of their years together.

"Well look at that, Anna. And I feel it too. I feel the connection! It's a Traveler and her horse. I can't wait to meet them. I feel it. Oh Anna, LET'S RIDE! *LET'S LET LOOSE AND RIDE*," cried Abby. "Let me run!"

"Okay then, I agree! Giddy up!" Anna cried, letting her reins go forward in her hand and giving a squeeze of her legs. "Let's run, I agree, let's run!" Anna cried again. "We can be elegant even if we run like mad. I agree; let's go!!"

The sun was shining brightly. Birds flew from little tufts of meadow grasses to other tufts. When they landed, sometimes the tufts of grasses waved back and forth with the weight of these tiny creatures. A marmot whistled.

And then those two seasoned Travelers tore off as fast as they could go!

CHAPTER NINETEEN

LIZA FINDS ANNA

Libby heard the piercing noise of a whinny, then heard the second and third whinny too. Her head perked up and her ears went forward with excitement.

Liza and Libby had been on the trails for a few days after their restful stay in the mountain hut. They had been told to look for the other Traveler and all they knew was to stick to the trails and to follow the signs whenever they could. So here they were, on the trails and they knew that someone was approaching. They hadn't met anyone in a long time and regardless, this loud call from the horse seemed unusual. Liza wasn't certain at first if she should be concerned.

But there was something about that whinny that was unique. There was an urgent persistence to the sound and yet it wasn't a sound of danger. Libby knew about danger and how horses would call to one another. One time, when Liza and her family had been out on horseback, her father's horse Dude had screamed a whinny of danger when he had come upon a rattlesnake. He had also stepped backwards very quickly so all the horses knew that something was wrong up ahead. But that wasn't the tone of the whinny that Libby had heard just now. This was something very different. It was a special call. Libby knew what it meant in an instant.

She called out as loudly as she could.

Libby had moved down into a dead stop and stood perfectly still with her front legs planted firmly into the ground. She had lifted her head and her nostrils were flaring. The wind was blowing a gentle breeze and with her stance and her mane flowing and her trail swishing back and forth, she looked magnificent. Anyone watching Libby's demeanor would have thought the same. She looked like a positively gorgeous mare at that moment. Every muscle quivered as she whinnied again and snorted through her flared nostrils.

"We're here! Liza, this is the moment! Liza, we are HERE!" Libby exclaimed. "I think we've found her. I think we've found her. I can see that far. I just know it's the Traveler we've been seeking. Oh wow!"

Liza looked out into the distance and simply sat, dumbfounded.

She had been enjoying all the days of travel and enjoying each and every one of her experiences with Libby. And while she knew to follow the signs, she had not made a plan what to do once she had found the other Traveler.

But who was that in the distance? Liza had never seen a reaction from Libby like this before. In all her years of competing with Libby and going on trail rides with Libby, and in all her travels this mare, she had never seen Libby stand so proudly and with such an air of confidence and determination. She looked beautiful!

Libby whinnied again. This time it was so loud it nearly pieced Liza's eardrums.

Liza's heart began to race. What was happening? Did they find the Traveler that Meia's family had described to her? Was this the person Liza was meant to find? Meia's mother was insistent to follow the signs and to find the other Traveler. And they had seen a few signs on their travels so far. Surely, the way Libby was reacting, this must be the other Traveler. And she was on horseback too. Liza could see by now that it was a woman!

But Liza wasn't prepared!

"What do I say? What do I do? Do I wait or have us walk forward? She's running so fast toward us. Should we just wait here?" Liza contemplated.

"I'm ready to run if you are, Liza," Libby said.

"Well then, let's run, Libby, let's run!" Liza cried. "As fast as you can and as fast as you want, let's run! It's the Traveler, I just know it!" exclaimed Liza.

CHAPTER TWENTY

TWO TRAVELERS

"Abby, you know, you'd better slow down because we will frighten her, surely," Anna cried out to Abby. "Just slow down please so I don't have to make you," Anna said again. Anna changed the way she sat down in the saddle and Abby instinctively changed her gait.

As Abby slowed, Anna could see the horse in the distance relax a bit too. Anna was certain this was the Traveler she had felt and she wanted to make a good impression.

"But she's just a child," Anna frowned. "She's just a young girl. Probably not even a teenager," Anna said to Abby. Anna was looking into the distance and determined that this Traveler was not an adult.

"How did such a young Traveler come through?" Anna asked Abby, as she felt Abby come down into a fast trot and then move down into a fast walk. Abby was breathing heavily and was excited but relaxed.

"Don't worry about it, Anna," Abby said. "It doesn't matter how old she is. I'm sure meeting up with her will be quite the experience for you and for her," Abby said.

"I haven't met someone who has come through recently in a long time," Anna mused. "I'll have to take my time to explain things to this young Traveler," she said.

"I'll help with that," said Abby.

Libby relaxed when she saw that the other horse had slowed its pace. "That's the way to make a proper greeting," Libby said with a laugh in her words. "None of this running up at a gallop! We are all meeting one another for the first time and everyone needs to stay calm," Libby added.

The young Traveler and her horse were on one side of the valley and the other Traveler and her horse were on the other side of the meadow of this long valley, all headed quite purposely toward one another, rapidly narrowing the distance.

"Hello," said Anna, as they got closer. Anna felt that warmth again. Abby made a gentle whinny and then a nicker and calmly walked right up to Libby and nuzzled her.

"Hello," said Liza. She noticed that Libby did not seem guarded at all and was nuzzling the other horse right back.

"We're both using English as our language," thought Liza.

Then there was a pause. The horses stood still and flicked their tails.

It was at this moment, that both riders looked closely at one another and immediately raised their eyebrows and opened their mouths in shock. Their expressions were identical.

"You're a cowgirl!" they both cried in unison.

I'M ANNA AND I'M LIZA

The two Travelers started laughing and pointing at one another and then their words began to tumble out of their mouths, and in their excitement, they realized they were speaking on top of one another.

"You go first," said Anna.

"No, ma'am, if you please, you go first," exclaimed Liza.

Anna used her reins to nudge Abby away from Libby just to give her a little space and once she got Abby settled, Anna said, "My name is Anna. I've been looking for you. And this is my horse Abby," Anna said.

"Pleased to meet you, Miss Anna. My name is Liza. I'm twelve and this is my horse Libby. We've been on the trails for a long time, hoping to find you, although we did not know what to expect," said Liza.

She noticed that Libby was listening intently but not saying a word.

Anna noticed that her normally chatty horse was also being quiet and respectful and very calm. She smiled at how unusual that was and decided to enjoy the moment.

"You seem as though you have been having a good time of it all here in this world," Anna said. Anna observed that Liza seemed very confident and at ease but then she noticed that Liza sat upright looking slightly shocked when Anna had said the words, 'this world'.

Anna also noticed that Liza's eyes casually traveled down to follow where Anna's hand had moved while they were sitting there on their horses. Anna had put the reins into her right hand and with her left, was holding out a circular wooden disc attached to a leather strap. Liza saw what was in Anna's hand and then Liza practically screamed, "The sign!" It was plain as day. Anna had the sign of the Traveler. Liza put her reins in her left hand and with her right, lifted up the disc that had been hanging from Libby's saddle horn. They were identical.

"I'm a Traveler, Liza. I am sure that you have heard something about me and that you have met a few people here in the mountains who know all about Travelers, because you have the sign. Was it given to you here in this world or given to you in your own world?" Anna asked.

Liza was shocked and also very relieved. Her journey was over. Well, kind of. Perhaps her journey was only beginning but at least Meia's mother was correct. There was another Traveler right here in the Alps and since they had followed the signs, Liza had found her. And the Traveler was a cowgirl! Liza could not believe it. A cowgirl!

But what would happen now? And what did Anna mean when she had just asked, "Was the sign given to you in your own world?" Liza would have to try to remember to ask Anna what she had meant by that.

"Actually," Anna said, "wait a moment. Let's give our horses a break and use the time to really meet one another and discuss our experiences. This has to be quite a shock for you and perhaps I can explain some things now that we have met one another," Anna said.

They both dismounted and took off their horses' bridles and then loosened their cinches. Liza had been casually taking careful notice of the kind of tack Abby had on and was taking inventory of all the clothing Anna was wearing. "Everything looks kind of like what I have," Liza noted. "I wonder if she is from my time? I need to be patient and let this story unfold. There has to be a story here and I need to just wait and allow Anna to tell me," Liza decided.

"Let's go on over here and let the horses graze. There is an outcropping of rocks and I don't know about you but I'm hungry and need some food," Anna said. "We can sit there and talk," she added.

"I'm hungry too," said Liza. She turned to Libby and said, "Come on girl. We are going to walk over here."

Libby replied, "Works for me. I can see that the grass looks much better over there. Mmmm, it IS better," said Libby.

"Race you to it," Abby challenged.

Anna laughed. "Horses," Liza and Anna said in unison and then they both laughed!

Liza noticed that Anna wasn't using a halter for Abby and Anna followed her gaze and said, "Neither Libby nor Abby need halters here in this world, do they?" Anna asked. "Haven't you noticed?" she continued.

"I have used it from time to time because I think most people would not understand a horse that wasn't under the control of a human," Liza said. "But not very often. Libby doesn't need it anymore. You're correct! She seems to know instinctively how far to stray while she grazes at night. Frankly, she does not stray far, that's for sure, now that I think about it. I think Libby is always trying to protect me so she does not stray far at all, ever, actually," said Liza. "In this world," she added.

"Abby is the same way now," said Anna.

"Who was this very interesting cowgirl?" thought Liza. "She seems very distinguished. She is very tall and she is very pretty," Liza observed.

"I'm from back East," said Liza. "We have a ranch but we go on the road with our horses a lot. And we compete with them. I was traveling with my parents and we were staying over in Arizona for the winter," Liza said and suddenly, she started to get tears in the corners of her eyes. So, she stopped talking. Liza noticed that Anna was a very good listener. She had kept quiet while Liza began to tell her story. Even when she got a little teary, Anna didn't coddle her, she noticed. She had remained focused on Liza and her story and nodded from time to time.

"And?" asked Anna.

"Well, I don't know if it happened to you too, the way it happened to me, that is, well, you know... one moment we were there, pretending and having fun running through the hills of Arizona and then boom, we were trotting on steep trails in the mountains of the Swiss Alps," said Liza. She noticed she had been speaking very quickly. Her mother was always trying to work with Liza on her elocution and to properly enunciate and to project words to an audience when speaking. She tried to tell herself to slow down and not to speak like a silly child. She was a proper pre-teen cowgirl and cowgirls knew how to present themselves!

"And then?" Anna asked patiently. "What happened after you came through?"

"Libby started speaking and I understood her!" cried Liza. At that, Libby lifted her head and made a loud nicker, and with the sun gleaming on her mane and back, Liza thought Libby looked very elegant, standing there in the sunlight.

Anna smiled. "That's about what happened to Abby when we came through. The only thing is that she doesn't stop talking, and hasn't stopped talking ever since we came through, I've noticed!" Anna said lightheartedly. "To tell the truth, she never stops!" she continued.

Liza saw Abby whip her head up out of the lush grass. The horse had such a funny look on her face, that Liza was thinking that the look on Abby's face at that moment was almost of a petulant child who was getting ready to stick out her tongue in jest.

"At first, I was scared and concerned," continued Liza. "Especially when I could not find the fog bank again."

"So, it was a fog bank for you, then, right?" Anna asked, politely interrupting, trying to clarify and understand how Liza had come through.

"Yes, we came through an unusual fog bank, and it disappeared right after we came through it." Liza paused. "But my Libby-girl was very helpful. I cried a little at first, then we just got right down to it and decided to have adventures together," Liza said. Her face was beaming right then. She was exhilarated and she was so happy. Anna saw the radiance of a smart, confident, beautiful young cowgirl and she just smiled.

By this time, the two cowgirls noticed that their horses had slowly made their way back close to their mistresses. It seemed they no longer felt the need to give their owners any more privacy. They wanted to be a part of it all now.

"Liza has been taking great care of me," Libby said.

"Anna made sure I had plenty to eat when we came through," Abby said.

"Liza took care of my stone bruise," Libby bantered right back.

"Anna takes me everywhere with her. Everywhere she goes, I go," Abby chimed in.

Liza and Anna began to laugh. "Libby won't win this competition to come up with the best story, you know," said Anna. "Abby will wear her out, I'm sure!"

"Oh, I don't know about that!" Libby said. If horses could laugh, Liza was sure Libby was laughing at all of this.

After a quiet moment, Anna continued. "How long have you been here?" asked Anna.

"I think it's been going on two or three weeks by now," said Liza. "It could be way more. I haven't been counting to be honest."

"And have you met some nice people?" Anna asked.

"My gift, this sign, this gift, well, we met a family shortly after we came through," Liza said. "They had two children, Balthazar and Meia," Liza continued.

Anna smiled and said knowingly, "Ah, so they named the child Meia. That's a lovely Swiss girl's name meaning 'strength'," she explained. She sat back on the rock they were on and looked out into the distance.

"When I met them, they were expecting and I did not know if would be a boy or a girl," Anna said pensively. "Tell me more about the boy," Anna said. "Do they call him Balthis?"

"Yes," said Liza. "He's a silly boy. You know boys. But I think he really liked the way Meia took to Libby. We were only there at their chalet in the little valley for a few days, but Meia really liked Libby and Balthis would tease us a bit the way boys do."

Anna smiled. "Go on," she prodded gently.

"I shouldn't really call him a silly boy. Let me correct myself. He is a very hard worker. He gets up early and takes the sheep up into the hills. He usually has a book with him and although he is quiet, there is something important about him. I could see that he was very kind and strong and very smart. He keeps his room neat and the stable even neater," Liza added.

"He loves his sister, even with the teasing, and he definitely loves his parents. He always had a bag with him, full of books, now that I think more about it. I think he might become a professor sometime, I wonder," said Liza.

Anna was smiling a lot at this. "Did the Father give you the gift of the sign?" she asked.

"The Father was very kind and gave me this gift," Liza said. "But hang on a minute, you know them really well then, is that right?" asked Liza.

Anna smiled a knowing smile. "I must have come through near to where you did. Just up the mountain from them. Somehow both of us stumbled upon the same family when we came through. Perhaps it's a good thing that happened. For me, when I arrived, Balthis was very ill with a fever. I stayed with the family until he was cured. I'm a doctor," Anna said.

"Ooooh, then I will call you Doctor Anna and not Miss Anna," Liza cried.

"Liza, you are certainly a polite young lady, that is for sure. 'Miss Anna' will be just fine," Anna chuckled. "But yes, I am a doctor and I came through at the time when the family needed someone like me the most. They live in a remote part of the Alps and Balthis probably would have died without my help," Anna said.

Suddenly Anna practically fell forward. Abby had snuck up directly behind her and nudged her gently and yet just enough to almost cause her to fall off the rock she was sitting on with Liza. She tousled Abby's mane and then rubbed Abby's cheeks. "Silly mare," Anna said. "Go eat some more grass. We have a lot of trails to cover and Liza and I have some more Traveler talk to catch up on," said Anna.

By this time, Libby had walked over to Liza and calmly put her nose down close to Liza and breathed on her. Liza felt those whiskers and she saw those beautiful eyes of her mare. Liza ran her hands up and down Libby's neck and played with her mane and then ran her hand over Libby's forelock and played with that a little bit.

"I think we are safe here, Libby-girl," Liza said.

"I do too," said Libby.

CHAPTER TWENTY-TWO

THE WATCHMAKER

"So, Liza, are you in any rush to get back? I can show you many interesting things while you are here if you would like," said Anna.

"I would love that," cried Liza.

Anna had a kind of mischievous look on her face and was pleased that Liza was up for more adventures.

"Well, I miss my parents and I am sure they are very worried about me but I've been gone so long already that I guess it wouldn't matter if I stayed a little longer," Liza said.

"Well," said Anna, "with just a few days of easy riding, we will be able to make it down to a much larger village where my toolmaker is located. He's actually a watchmaker but he fashions special precision tools for me," said Anna.

"Tools?" asked Liza.

"I'm sure you know from your studies Liza, that the Swiss have always been truly excellent craftsmen. Their workmanship and millwork and precision metalwork is unparalleled," said Anna.

After their meeting in the meadow, they had gotten back on their horses and started walking through the valley as they made their plans.

The horses were walking along with their ears at attention. They weren't talking to one another but instead both were listening carefully to their riders. Their ears were moving this way and that as the conversation proceeded.

Libby was confident that her mistress was safe and secure riding with and being with Anna. At the same time, she wanted to be certain that all future plans sounded safe.

"I'd like to show you something, Liza," said Anna. As they rode, she reached down into her bag and pulled out a metal instrument that looked like a long pair of tweezers. There were various screws and clamping gadgets as a part of it and the entire tool and its components looked like it had been made with the utmost care.

"My watchmaker friend made these for me. I use these in special surgical situations. This one will need to be sterilized of course, before I use it again. Here, please take a look," Anna said. She held it out to Liza for her to see.

Libby was listening so she knew instinctively to move her body closer to Abby without Liza having to put a leg on her side to guide her. Libby was tempted to be polite and wait to be asked to move over but she didn't think Liza would mind that she was listening in on the conversation of the two cowgirls.

"This is beautiful work," cried Liza. "It's been made especially for you in this world or did you bring it with you?" Liza asked.

"That's what I want to show you, Liza."

"Will Libby have safe places to stay along the road we are taking? If we are going into larger villages, we look so different and we act so differently. I just want Libby to be safe. I suppose I'm more worried about her than I am about myself," Liza said laughing nervously.

Libby nickered. "We like to take care of one another, that's for sure," Libby said. "But thank you, Liza, for always thinking of me."

Liza leaned forward and stroked Libby on her neck and gave her a pat on her withers.

"Please don't worry at all," said Anna. "I have lived here for a long time now. I have many friends all along the trails and paths and roads where I travel. They look out for me and they pass word along once they realize that I am coming by their villages. They are like my new family," Anna said. "Some know my past, but not all of course."

Libby shook her head and said, "May I say something, Liza? I have a comment to make."

"Of course, girl."

"Well, since we began this adventure, I've been enjoying myself. All the grasses and some of the grains in the different grasses are keeping me healthy and strong. We have been walking, trotting and loping quite a lot and you already had me in shape, so, I'm only getting stronger every day. There has been fresh water all along our travels. So as you might guess, I am very happy to continue along with you for sure," said Libby. She paused, clearly deep in thought. Then she said, "I say, let's go!"

Libby tossed her head with happiness and did a little trotting dance for a moment as she said this then settled back into her steady walk.

Abby whinnied. "I'm always up for being on these trails. You know that Anna!"

"Anna, Libby told me after we came through the fog bank that I would have very special and unique experiences here. And that I should take advantage of all of them. So, yes, if you don't mind, I'd like to learn new things and stay here with you," Liza declared.

"Then let's take this trail that swings back and heads toward the tree line out of the meadow," Anna said. And off they went.

For the first two days of traveling together, the two cowgirls had spent a lot of time at an easy walking pace with their horses and just talked. Anna was very interested to learn about Liza's life and lifestyle as well as the competitions she and Libby had been in. Anna enjoyed hearing about Liza's family, her studies and the books she liked to read.

The trails were becoming consistently wider the more the cowgirls descended into the valleys below. Up higher, the trails were narrow and more for single file. Sometimes they were a little more worn when the trail was closer to a small cluster of chalets, but for the most part, two riders had to ride single file.

Deeper into the lower valleys, they were able to ride side by side all the time. These trails were almost like roads; more suitable for carts or wagons.

Each day they encountered more people and walked past more mountain huts and the lower they went, they went by chalets. Instead of seeing one hut at a time, they saw four. Instead of seeing two chalets at a time, they saw eight or ten.

Looking off into the distance, Liza could see they were coming upon a much larger village. More like a small town she thought, but it was a village none the less.

Liza was slightly concerned. In the beginning of her adventures with Libby, they had come upon one person or one family at a time and it was easy to dodge odd looks or to deflect questions. Now, amongst more people, she might be asked even more personal and probing questions. Should she answer them or leave it all up to Anna? What would she experience being in a small town?

She knew that she looked different from other people. It wasn't just the cultural differences between the Swiss and herself as a Western cowgirl. It was differences in the time period. And, though slight, Liza knew she definitely did not look local and of this time period.

At one point Anna asked her about this.

"Liza, you aren't worried that people will ask many questions, are you?" Anna asked.

"Well, of course I am," Liza replied.

"I thought so. You were quiet these past few hours and as the town came into view, I presumed that you were thinking in your head that you are going to be noticed and that you're not going to know how to handle it. You are a very mature twelve-year-old, but you are still young and I can perceive that you are nervous. Don't be, Liza," Anna said kindly.

"Well I am wearing an unusual cowboy hat. And I wear my hair differently as well. My jacket is different, my jeans are unusual with the cowgirl bling, my saddle and saddle packs are all made differently and even made with modern material. So I am a little nervous," said Liza.

"Do you feel that you need to fit in?" Anna asked with a quizzical yet mischievous look on her face. Liza had noticed that Anna was patient, kind, helpful and caring and Liza had felt very comfortable with her new cowgirl mentor these past few days.

In anticipation of meeting a Traveler who might have been unprepared, Anna had packed extra items including a spare bedroll, which certainly came in handy. During their travels, they had laid out their bedrolls under the stars and had made a little campfire each evening to take away the nighttime chill in the air. They had talked a lot about being cowgirls and being Travelers. Liza had already asked Anna a few times how people had reacted to her being here, and Anna had told her frankly that she did not worry about it.

But today, Liza felt she needed a little courage. Even still, she instinctively knew the answer to Anna's question.

"I don't need to fit in," Liza said decisively. "I don't mind looking different. I have just decided that I'm fine and can't wait to meet more local people," Liza said with confidence. Libby made what seemed to be a head nod of approval and agreement.

133

Liza began to notice that as they descended, the number of chalets wasn't the only change, but rather, at the lower elevation, the gardens were larger. She knew they were still up high in the Alps, but Liza could see that every chalet down here had a very large garden. And the chalets themselves were much larger. Some were three and four stories tall. And beautiful!

It seemed that every level of the chalets had balconies and from each balcony rail hung boxes full of flowers. The boxes were all very large and long, and each and every one of them in this town was bursting with beautiful flowers draping over the edges of the railings. All the windows of each room of the chalets had white lace hanging in them and also had a separate set of curtains pulled back on the sides of each window.

Liza could not get over how colorful everything was against the backdrop of those very dark wooden chalets. She also noticed that while everyone in this town seemed hard at work, they all had taken time to keep their homes neat and tidy and festooned with these colorful flowers. Even their gardens had rows of flowers in them as well as vegetables to eat. It was all quite idyllic.

After following the road into the edge of town, Anna stopped their little group in front of a shop. Liza looked at the front door and then continued her gaze up to look at the sign above it that was hanging from a wrought iron hook. As she looked up at the sign for the shop, Liza gasped.

"The sign, it has, well, this shop has the Traveler sign engraved in it!" she cried out to Anna. Liza looked down at the gift of the small wooden carved disc that she carried attached to her own saddle horn and then she looked back up at the sign engraved here hanging in front of the shop.

"Is this how you know you are amongst friends?" Liza asked Anna.

Anna smiled. "But of course!" she exclaimed.

The cowgirls dismounted and Anna showed Liza where to lead the two horses to the back of the shop for them to stand peacefully and relax. There was a bucket of water already hanging for the horses, and Abby and Libby were happy to gulp some down. Loosening the cinches and removing the bridles, Liza and Anna put halters on Libby and Abby and let their lead ropes drop to the ground.

Then the cowgirls removed the rest of the tack and stored it in the stable nearby.

"We know they won't go anywhere!" Anna laughed. "But I always put a halter on Abby when we are in larger villages and towns so she doesn't look out of place," Anna said. "They can graze here in the grass. They'll be fine."

Suddenly a noise startled Liza, and she quickly looked behind her.

"I was wondering when you would come to see me, Doctor Anna, I mean Miss Anna," a man's voice cried. The man had come out of the back of the chalet and while wiping his hands on a towel, he was walking enthusiastically towards the cowgirls. "I had gotten word you were on your way and every day I kept the water fresh for your horses. How are you my friend?" he said to Anna, giving Abby a pat and a rub.

Abby gave a gentle nicker of hello and as for Anna, she gave the man a hug. Then they kissed one another several times on each cheek as a part of their greeting.

He was a tall man, though shorter a bit than Anna. He wore a white shirt with rolled sleeves. While his dark trousers looked newer and more modern than those of the men in the hills, they were similar in style. As with most men, his had evidence of being neatly pressed. He was wearing a leather industrial apron, and Liza noticed that several pair of spectacles were tucked into two of his many pockets. The apron looked specially made for him.

Liza looked at the man's hands. This was a man who worked with his hands but they did not have the rough look of the hands of the men in the mountains. Rather, his hands with their long fingers had the look of a pianist and though worn, looked like they worked with intricate tools. He was wearing an additional pair of magnifying glasses that made him look like the jewelry repairman her family knew back home.

"Come inside, ladies, come inside," he said in a welcoming voice. He stood to the side of the path and opened his arms wide, to guide them towards the back door of the chalet.

"I'm Liza," said Liza in a confident manner, beaming a broad smile toward the Watchmaker. "And that's my horse, Libby," she added.

"Welcome, my dear," the Watchmaker said. "A warm welcome to you and your horse," he added.

Once inside, Liza was astounded.

"Miss Anna, come over here and see what I have made for you since your last visit," he cried with enthusiasm. "Come here, come here," he added.

Liza had noticed that the deep respect the man had for Anna had not diminished when he corrected himself from calling her Doctor Anna and instead used the friendly but formal and respectful version of Miss Anna. There was a professional camaraderie here, Liza was certain of that. As she watched them, Liza was enjoying all of this.

Anna walked over to a workbench and as she did, Liza looked around the workshop and noticed all the sketches and samples of the man's craftsmanship. Such detail and such work! This was more than a watchmaker; this was an industrial designer who clearly loved his work. There were pieces of metal of all shapes and sizes hanging down from hooks on the walls. And various kinds of equipment to hold and shape the various metals were situated all around the workshop. All kinds of intricate specialty tools hung neatly in their place. Screwdrivers of every style, tools to shape and scrape and bend and twist and polish hung all around his workbench. An oddly shaped circular device with levers, clamps and screws was surrounded by watch parts, laid out in an organized fashion on a large piece of green baize.

Liza was enjoying witnessing the camaraderie of her cowgirl friend with the Watchmaker, and she was admiring all of the sketches.

She noticed that all of them were of surgical and medical tools. She was absolutely astounded. Was Anna an inventor? Was the man an inventor? Were they partners in something? Or were they involved in a business venture perhaps?

"Miss Liza, come over here would you please," said the Watchmaker politely. "Let me look at you. May I?"

"Yes sir, that would be fine," said Liza.

"Ah yes, a Traveler," he said. Liza's eyes widened.

"I saw the engraving on your sign out front, sir," Liza said, "so I knew I was safe here."

"Yes, my dear. We speak freely here and you should have no worries," the Watchmaker said.

Anna nodded. "We work together, the Watchmaker and I," she said.

Liza just observed everything and wanted this moment to unfold without asking too many questions. The Watchmaker and Anna put their heads together looking at sketches and then back at the examples of specialty tools and instruments that the Watchmaker had made. Liza could see that some of the sketches had been made in a woman's writing style and that some had the angular look of the Watchmaker's European handwriting style. All of the sketches had dimensions and comments noted on them. Liza noticed that the sketches looked like what you might see in a professional designer's office back home.

These two were clearly close professional friends. It was such a thrill to watch them working together and brainstorming and coming up with new ideas as they chatted.

"I was so intrigued by the drawing you gave me last time, Miss Anna, and I got a few more ideas of my own to enhance it. Look at this sample, this prototype. Will it work for you?" he asked thoughtfully.

"Oh my!" said Anna. "It's even better than I thought it could be," she exclaimed.

"I'm very anxious for you to test it and to please let me know if it will work for you. As you instructed, I also made additional samples for us to send to our trusted colleagues for them to test as well," the Watchmaker said.

Anna looked the specimen over carefully and held it this way and that. She held it in her left hand and then in her right, moving it to and fro. She nodded and smiled in approval.

"I see no reason why we can't go ahead and make more," said Anna. "It's incredible. I can see that already."

CHAPTER TWENTY-THREE

HOMESICK

The more Liza observed the interactions between Anna and the Watchmaker, the more Liza began to feel something starting to overwhelm her. She looked around at the workshop and continued to listen and process the excitement in the voices of these two colleagues.

Then Liza realized what she was feeling. She had become slightly homesick.

She could see that these were two professionals, who had mutual respect and admiration for one another. And in some ways, that's what her parents had. They had love for one another and that was definitely different from the relationship that the Watchmaker had with Anna. But the pleasant and friendly way that they bantered and conversed, made her miss her parents. They were like that too and Liza felt terribly lonely for a moment.

She excused herself and stepped outside and went over to the horses. She gathered their lead ropes and guided them into the stable. She gave them hay and then she began to curry first Abby and then Libby. The horses ate their hay and remained quiet.

"I miss Mama and Papa," Liza finally said.

Libby was quiet. Abby had pricked her ears up and was moving them back and forth listening politely as she ate hay. But she didn't want to appear to eavesdrop, so she kept her head down.

"I really miss them," Liza said again.

"We can return you know. Nothing is keeping you here," Libby said. "I will gladly do as you please," Libby said nuzzling Liza. "We can head right back on all those trails and look for the fog bank in the mountains," Libby urged. "I'm happy to help you get back home to our world anytime you want to return," she said.

Liza did what she always did when she needed comfort. She threw her arms about Libby and hugged her. Pressing her head against Libby's neck, Liza inhaled and just breathed in Libby's scent. She took another deep breath through her nose several times which calmed her. Abby lifted her head and slowly moved closer to the pair.

"I like having you two here, you know," said Abby. "I think this adventure is good for Anna, but Liza you have to do what is right for you," continued Abby. Abby arched her neck and lowered her nose and curled herself into the mix that was Libby and Liza. She just stood there with the two of them and for a moment, Abby was glad she could help.

After a few minutes of this, Liza felt much better. Her breathing relaxed as she enjoyed the company of the two horses.

When Abby realized that Liza was feeling better, she lifted her head and took a step back from them.

"You know," she said, "Anna had a hard time here at first. She was very homesick and yet also very happy to be here. She felt needed here and she found a sense of purpose. Do you know what that means, Liza?" Abby asked.

"A sense of purpose?" asked Liza.

"Yes," said Abby.

"I think I do," Liza said, "but I'm not sure."

Abby continued. "Well, toward the end, Anna wasn't totally happy in her world. I'm certain she will tell you everything that happened in her own way and when she is ready. All I can tell you is that once she got here, she was very conflicted about remaining here or going back. She wasn't sure whether to stay and explore and then go back, or whether to stay and make a new home here. I was with her during all of those big decisions. We made them together. I spent a lot of my time listening to her, even though here in this world, we could communicate quite easily," Abby said.

"I believe I understand, at least I think so," said Liza thoughtfully.

"After a while, Anna found a reason to stay. She set goals and built meaningful relationships," Abby said. "This is what I meant when I said that Anna had finally found a true sense of purpose," explained Abby.

They all stood quietly as though they had heard something important that required a respectful moment or two of polite and contemplative silence.

"Thank you, Abby," Liza said after a few moments. "I'm still missing my parents but I think everything will be okay. I have Libby and we are on a very interesting and also unbelievable adventure, and I want to continue."

"Good for you, Liza," said Libby. "And I will be with you every step of the way."

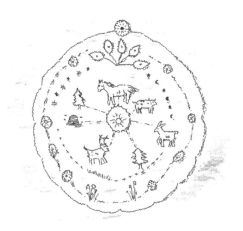

CHAPTER TWENTY-FOUR

GO DO GREAT THINGS

"Come, let us make dinner and get you settled," said the Watchmaker. He appeared to be a happy man and had a twinkle of kindness in his eyes.

He took off his working glasses and pulled out a handkerchief and wiped his face gently. Placing his glasses into another pocket of his apron, he undid the clasp at the top and carefully removed it. Then he hung it on an ornate handmade hook at the exit of the workshop.

"One who sculpts metal for others must also make the time to craft clever objects for himself," the Watchmaker chuckled as he hung up his apron.

As they walked from the workshop into his home, Liza felt like she had walked into the home of a true book-lover. All over the shelves were books, books and more books! Liza saw books on history, geography, metalworking, mining, and culture.

"Oh look, Mark Twain," Liza commented. "You have books from the United States," she continued. "And here is a book by George Washington, too!"

"It takes a little while for books to make it here to our village so these two are relatively new," the Watchmaker said. "But I have a nice library down the hall."

Liza smiled a knowing smile at Anna.

"All right you two," the Watchmaker said. "I saw that. Come let's eat."

He had set the table adding a place for Liza. After a quick wash of her hands and face, she realized she was very hungry.

The table was set with fresh breads, fresh cheeses, new butter, a pitcher of milk and a plate of various meats. The Watchmaker ladled out some hearty soup for the cowgirls as well. After a blessing, they dug in. It was a friendly meal as they told stories of being on the trails and sleeping under the stars.

"I don't think anyone ever gets used to rocks and pebbles underneath them when they have to rough it," said Anna.

"Trust me, little girls don't like it either," laughed Liza.

When the meal ended, Liza offered to clean everything up and to go give more water to the horses.

Anna and the Watchmaker used the free time to go back into the shop and huddle over sketches and samples and they discussed even more ideas for new tools and pieces of equipment. After cleaning up from the dinner and watering the horses, Liza wandered back into the workshop and she watched them hard at work, marveling at it all.

Liza excused herself with a slight clearing of her throat and interrupted them for just a moment. "Excuse me," Liza said. "But you have such a beautiful home. Would you mind if I looked around, especially in your library, sir?"

"Not at all, my dear," the Watchmaker said.

Liza went back into the chalet and strolled through the hallway on the other side of the dining room. She passed a beautiful clock in a wooden case on top of a piece of furniture. As she walked down the hall, she could see the large doorway of what she guessed must be the library. Liza loved books so this room would be like a little slice of heaven for her. When Liza walked into the room, something caught her attention that startled her.

There, hanging on the wall, was the portrait of an absolutely beautiful woman, whose beauty was captured in this stunning near life-sized oil painting.

As Liza moved in closer, she saw the beautiful smile on the woman's face. She was clearly a happy person. No artist could paint such a smile unless the original subject was glowing with pure joy such as this woman evidently was.

In the one corner of the room near the painting, Liza saw something even more incredible. It was a piano. It was sleek and black and polished to perfection. On top, Liza could see a couple of photographs nestled into ornate silver frames, each with swirls and detailed patterns.

As Liza looked closer, she saw that one of the photos was of the woman whose portrait was hanging on the wall. And then Liza saw another photo with the Watchmaker, the woman, and a young girl about the same age as herself.

"There is a story here," Liza said to herself. "There has got to be a story as to why he seems to live alone yet has evidence of family everywhere. Hmmm."

"This man has a family," Liza said out loud. "I wonder where they are? It's late and they should be home by now," she postulated.

Liza moved away from the piano and scoured the shelves looking at all the leatherbound books with thick heavy spines and gold inlaid printing. The books appeared to be in at least four different languages. Liza knew a few of the words and without even removing any books from the shelves knew that there were many on the topics of history, philosophy, religion and medicine. This enigmatic and fascinating Watchmaker seemed quite the interesting character for sure and Liza already felt glad to know him.

Liza heard a sound of creaking wood behind her and turned to look.

"I see that you have discovered my beloved family," said the Watchmaker. The twinkle in his eye looked dimmed ever so slightly, Liza observed. Perhaps it was only the lighting.

But the Watchmaker walked over to the piano and picked up one of the framed photos and smiled jubilantly at the photo. He was clearly very proud.

"Miss Anna is still working in the workshop and I thought you might have some questions based on what you would find here in the library," he said.

"I do," said Liza. "Is this your family?" she asked.

"It certainly is," said the Watchmaker. "Would you like to hear the story?" he asked. He was smiling.

"Of course," said Liza.

"The story I'm going to tell you includes one of the most difficult decisions I've ever had to make but I have come to realize that it was a very good one," he began. "This all happened shortly after I met Miss Anna and learned all about her work. I had heard stories about her up and down the valley and even more stories were passed along from people in other valleys. I was very eager to meet her." The Watchmaker paused.

"Let me correct myself. *WE* were eager to meet her. My wife and daughter both wanted to meet Miss Anna. When she came here we were introduced to one another by a colleague. My wife and I invited her here to dinner. My family was very impressed by her. No, permit me to correct myself. We were all very *inspired* by her. Here she was, a woman, by herself going out and doing what was traditionally and typically a man's work. She was traveling without any worry or care and she was doing it all by herself. With her horse, of course!" he added with a twinkle. "Always with her beloved Abby."

Liza smiled and laughed a little.

"Regardless, we realized she was very accomplished. My daughter was really taken with her. She's your age, Liza, I'm sure. Miss Anna would come here frequently, and gradually she became more comfortable with us and shared her entire story. If she hasn't told you her story, I am sure she will, by the way," he continued.

"The more we all got to know her, as I mentioned, the more we realized that we were also deeply inspired by her. So much so that my wife and I wanted to take a big step for our daughter to improve her life. This was to enhance the passion in her and to afford her a special future. Anna inspired us to understand how wonderfully a passion can be turned into something amazing and we wanted that for our daughter. You see, she is a very accomplished pianist, especially for her age. And after much discussion and based on the financial successes of the equipment I was able to sell, my wife and I made a very important decision."

"What was that?" Liza asked, transfixed.

"We decided that the two of them – my wife and my daughter - would travel the continent so our daughter could study with the great pianists of our time. I'm sure you can imagine if you know a little bit about history that young girls don't always get the chance to go out and do great things. My wife and I always wanted opportunities for our daughter and we decided to take this great leap after we both met Miss Anna."

Liza was very impressed.

The Watchmaker added to his story. "My wife and daughter have been gone for almost six months now, and based on the letters we have exchanged, this was the right thing to do. We're going to continue to do everything we can to encourage this great passion and talent in our daughter. She's the one who wants all of this; she wants to learn and we are encouraging her," he continued. He looked down at the photo, still in his hands, and smiled.

"Liza," he said.

"Yes, sir."

"Liza, I'm sure you are feeling this amazing connection with Miss Anna. And I'm already able to tell that you must have wonderful parents. You're a very bright, intelligent, compassionate and curious young lady. Your parents must be very proud of you and it's obvious that they encourage you to do great things," the Watchmaker said. Then he paused again.

Liza waited.

"Make sure that you indeed go and do great things, Liza. You're a Traveler and I know what that means. So you have been blessed with the opportunity to see and learn and experience and also to teach. You and your wonderful horse, Libby, are in the middle of a beautiful journey. And I hope that all of this inspires you to do all kinds of great things when you return to your world someday."

The Watchmaker turned his gaze to the portrait on the wall. Then he turned and looked back down at the photo in his hands. He looked up at Liza and nodded. He knew that she knew how powerful a moment this was.

"I must do great things," Liza said. "I *will* do great things!"

Liza thanked the Watchmaker and thought, "This has been quite the evening. Wow, what an evening!"

She strolled through the chalet admiring the other paintings on the walls of his home, and she spent some time examining the beautiful and dainty colorful porcelain figurines on various tabletops. Then she had an urge to check the horses one last time just to say goodnight.

When Liza got outside, she saw Anna coming back from the horses on the little path in between the workshop and the stable. They both stopped and Anna asked, "Going to check on Libby?"

"Yes, I am," said Liza. "I always do!" she added.

"I do that too," Anna said. "I always check on Abby and say good night. Every night! I think she would open the door and come find me if I didn't," Anna said with a laugh.

Liza walked over to the horses and saw that there was a little bit of silliness going on with the two of them.

"I smell peppermint," Liza exclaimed. "Who has the peppermint candy?" Liza asked in a mock scolding voice.

Both horses pursed their lips together somewhat, and mumbled and looked at one another with guilty looks on their faces, and then looked back at Liza. No one said anything. Then Liza heard a secretive crunch and looked back and forth between the two of them, trying to figure out who was eating and crunching on peppermints.

Both horses stood still, looking as guilty as ever, but neither of them confessed.

"I can smell them, you know," Liza said with a twinkle in her eye. "So at least tell me this. Are there any more candies?"

"Mmmmmf mmmm mmf mmf," said Libby.

"Busted!" Liza said. "You!"

"Look to your left in the bowl," Abby admitted. "The Watchmaker brought out a bowl earlier and made us promise not to eat them all up," she added.

"You two smell delicious!" Liza said, as she picked up a peppermint candy and popped one in her mouth.

So as the day came to a close, had anyone been walking by the little stable, they would have heard loud crunching, silly laughter and the sounds of contented horses.

The following day, after finalizing details of the next steps with some of the medical instruments, Liza and Anna got the horses ready and mounted up.

"I will see you in a few months," Anna said to the Watchmaker. "All the best to your wife and daughter," she added. "Please keep me posted on your daughter's progress and her many adventures. Perhaps her travels will inspire her to compose some of her own music!"

"I will, Miss Anna, I will. And it has been lovely meeting you too, my dear," the Watchmaker said as he turned to face Liza. He had his hand on Libby's nose and was gently stroking it. Libby's eyes were closed, of course, Liza noticed.

"Off we go," said Anna.

"Goodbye," Liza said. "Thank you for everything. And thank you for the peppermints," she added, grabbing one from her pocket and popping it in her mouth.

CHAPTER TWENTY-FIVE

I WAS MARRIED

It took about a week on the trails, but Anna and Liza had finally made their way to Anna's village. Liza was in awe of all the bustle of activity. There were carts laden with goods and hay going everywhere. People were on the street actively engaged in work. Here and there, two people stood chatting and catching up on local news, Liza presumed. She saw bread shops, meat shops, general repair shops, and one shop that only made shoes. She also saw a pastry and chocolate shop that looked so delicious it made her mouth water.

When they arrived at Anna's chalet, they let the horses out into Abby's pasture after storing the tack and giving the horses a good rubdown.

Both horses promptly flopped to their knees and rolled onto their backs. They rolled this way and that and kicked their legs into the air like horses do sometimes. Then they rolled one more time and got up and shook. Libby looked up and down the valley and then like any horse would do, walked straight over to the greenest grass she could find and began to eat.

Anna brought Liza into her chalet and Liza looked this way and that and admired everything. During their travels, Anna had explained some of her hobbies like painting, embroidery and woodworking, and Liza could see evidence of her passions being put to good use throughout the chalet.

"There is a spare room upstairs for you to put your things," Anna said. "Just up those stairs straight ahead. Turn left at the top."

Liza made her way up the steep wooden steps and into the pretty little guest room. Like Meia's room and the guest room at the Watchmaker's home, the bed had a fluffy down comforter on it with large square down pillows at the head of the bed. These guest pillows of Anna's were embroidered with geometric designs in various shades of reds, browns and beiges. Liza admired the hand-embroidered items then put her things down on a chair and walked to the windows.

Mmmmmm, everything smelled so fresh and clean, she noticed. She looked out the windows and admired the pretty window boxes. She looked into the distance at all of the other chalets there in the valley and marveled at the beauty of it all. "I still can't believe I'm here." And she flopped down on the bed and took a good stretch and a short rest.

Lying there, Liza thought back to her conversation with the Watchmaker. She thought about her parents, and Anna and the people she had met so far in this world.

"I can be anything I want," she exclaimed. "And I do need to take advantage of every experience I am having here and the experiences I'll have when I'm back in my own world."

Liza thought about what it would take to become a doctor, an entrepreneur, a veterinarian, an archeologist, a scientist, an explorer, or a painter. "Everything is possible. So many things are inspiring me right now."

When Liza came back downstairs, she found Anna busy in the kitchen preparing some snacks and drinks for them.

Looking at Anna who had her back to Liza at the moment, suddenly Liza blurted out a question.

After a pause, Anna's simple reply to Liza's question was, "Why yes, I was married."

Anna had said this softly.

Liza and Anna had just spent a wonderful day together riding, learning even more about Anna's life here in this world. Now, Abby and Libby were frolicking in the pasture together. Sometimes they rolled, sometimes they stood and looked into the distance and sometimes they dropped their heads and simply ate grass.

When they did, they were no more than ten feet apart from one another, Liza had noticed. At this moment, each of them had one leg in front of their bodies and their heads were down eating grass. Every now and then they would both raise their heads at the same time. Then they would take a step forward, switching front legs and drop their heads once again and munch away. Watching them, Liza was certain they were also carrying on various conversations.

Now, here in the wooden home with Anna, Liza felt more comfortable to ask about more serious topics. Anna had made some tea and added some of her own honey to each cup and they were slowly sipping away. Some apple slices, cheese and delicious cookies were on the table and Liza had eaten a few of the cookies, of course. They had chatted about this and that and about the goings-on at Anna's small farm but Liza had finally asked Anna the question she had been yearning to ask.

"Were you ever married?" Liza had asked.

Anna walked over to the table, casually sat down in her chair, then slowly sat back and placed her hands calmly on the table. She paused.

"I was happily married and we had always talked about having children together," Anna said matter of fact.

"We planned to have two children. A boy and a girl," she added.

"What happened?" asked Liza. She was really curious now. "Do you have children? How many do you have? Where are they? And where is your husband?"

The look on Anna's face told Liza everything she needed to know and Liza almost regretted asking Anna any of those questions. She knew instantly she could not take any of them back

"My husband worked on oil rigs and I had my medical career. School, residency, then I was fully into my work. We were both very happy pursuing our passions. We were often apart from one another and yet when we were both home, we had a very happy marriage and an active life together. And I had Abby, of course."

Anna paused. Liza watched her very carefully and suddenly, a sad chill ran through her as she analyzed Anna's facial expressions.

"One day I got a phone call that his oil rig had exploded. I was one of the first to learn about the accident. That news sent shivers down my spine because I knew that the next thing I was going to hear was that my husband had died."

Liza sat very still now. She focused her attention completely on Anna.

"There was very little that could help me with my grief. Even my time with Abby wasn't helping and I could tell that she knew I was in pain. But I turned to her more and more frequently and one time, finally, I just took some time off from work.

Abby and I went riding up into the hills every single day. We rode for hours. I started to feel better. One day, very early in the morning, I put on my favorite Western shirt and one of my trophy buckles. I don't know why I did that. We went back out onto the trails. The sun was just starting to rise. We were coming up over a crest and the sun was beginning to shine on my face and warm me up completely. And suddenly my grief turned into joy. I remember sitting very relaxed in my saddle at this point."

Liza continued to watch Anna's face as she relived her experience.

"With the sun on my face, something was happening to me that was turning my soul inside out and I felt a sense of calmness and happiness again. I also felt a tingling sensation that I could not understand. Abby and I were walking up a hill and as I felt the sun and the tingling in my body, I closed my eyes. I felt Abby's body through the saddle as she was walking underneath me."

Anna closed her eyes, remembering the moment.

"Abby was walking steadily and I felt the sun and we walked like that for a while. I was crying and smiling at the same time. It was like my soul was trying to find the truth, and on horseback, as you know, anything is possible."

Liza smiled and looked out the window into the pasture at Libby. She noticed that both horses had their heads up now, turned to the house, with their ears forward. They both were standing very still, watching and listening. Their nostrils were flaring and Liza knew they both had heard every word of Anna's story, even from where they were standing in the pasture.

"When I finally opened my eyes, I found myself in this place. I was in this new world, or perhaps I should call it this old world, here up in the Alps. Possibly where you came through. I can't be sure. After we came through, Abby spoke to me and I felt the same sense of confusion as you did when you first heard Libby speak, surely, but I was also so thrilled to have a friend again. And it was wonderful to be able to speak with someone who really understood me. You felt that way when Libby spoke to you for the first time, right Liza?" Anna asked.

"Yes, I sure did!" Liza replied excitedly.

"Only another Traveler with her horse understands how all of that feels," Anna added as she reflected back on that time in her life, long ago.

"Once I figured out what was going on and what time period it was, I stopped questioning everything. I didn't even try to go back. Abby and I traveled on and on and enjoyed everyone we met along the way. We explored for months and months," Anna said.

She paused for a moment.

"Early on when I first came through, I came across a hamlet that was far from any village and there was a little boy about your age who was very sick. By luck, I had some medicines in my saddlebag and I was able to take care of him. I can't tell you how happy that made me. That was Balthis. So, Abby and I kept traveling and I had the opportunity to help more people."

"People spoke of the news of this tall woman and her buckskin horse. They spoke about the woman who was dressed oddly and had strange horse tack, and stories about me spread through the Alps. Sometimes people would wait for me to arrive. They knew I was coming. My medicines would help people and sometimes I had to stitch up wounds and such. I was also able to diagnose ailments and encourage people to go to the clinics in the bigger cities."

Liza was awestruck.

"When I came through," Anna continued, "I was wearing my engagement ring and my wedding ring as well as some valuable earrings. Once I decided to stay, I resolved to put them to good use. I was able to quietly sell those to establish my home and my farm here. Also, using the knowledge that I had from our world, I was able to work with some very discrete Swiss craftsmen and women and high-quality metalworkers and other experts. We worked to design and make some special tools and instruments that have helped me in my medical practice." Anna paused.

"You met the Watchmaker. He is one of several with whom I work. They are sensible colleagues, interested in truth and goodness and knowledge. We make some money, of course, but no one is taking advantage of the fact that I am from another world and from another time. We just want to help people live," Anna continued.

Liza nodded. She was beginning to understand everything with much more clarity.

Then Anna said, "I had to be very careful not to scare anyone with what I knew. But it has been very helpful that's for sure. We made more tools and equipment and I was quietly able to sell those in several countries, not just here."

Liza was smiling at this part of the story. Anna had found a way to turn tragedy into triumph!

But Liza was curious too. "Was there a network of Travelers with their horses? There were people with the signs who knew all about them, but were there many more? And if so, where were they all? How many Traveler pairs had come through?" she wondered.

As Liza thought about all of this, she listened as Anna continued her story.

"These craftsmen and women were quite astonished, but no one questioned how I knew what I knew. I'm very happy here now and enjoy that I am needed and that I have a purpose. I have my local friends, I have friends in different countries through my medical work and I have healthy patients all over. I love my garden and this chalet and this little farm. And of course, I have Abby. I have been here for almost ten years and I have no regrets."

While Anna was telling her story, both Libby and Abby had come up to the open window and had been standing quietly outside. One of them made a gentle nicker and an audible sigh and Anna and Liza turned to look at them. They both smiled at their horses.

"Abby doesn't seem to age very quickly here at all I've noticed," said Anna, looking directly at her four-legged friend. "We are both alive here, in this very real place, in this new point in time, and I age normally but Abby ages more slowly. I can't explain it. From the looks of things, it almost seems as though we are paired in our life together now. And that when my life is over, Abby will be aged in sync with me somehow, as vibrant as ever though, and will be with me until the end. From what I can tell," said Anna thoughtfully.

Liza immediately stood up and had a look of shock on her face. And she got tremendously excited. "Do you mean if I stay here that Libby will live forever?" she cried. "That she and I will be together forever?" Liza asked passionately. She was looking very excited and genuinely happy at this thought. "To have Libby with me forever would be a dream come true," she said.

"No, Liza," Anna said. "Not exactly. Think back on what I said."

Liza got a moment of clarity and said, "Not forever. I understand. But her life would be tied to mine. I would never ever have to say goodbye to her though if she and I stayed here together in this world, right?" Liza said.

Anna did not reply. She allowed Liza a few moments to come to understand what it means to make a choice like this. Anna knew that it was important for Liza to weigh the outcomes of a decision and to understand both the benefits and the consequences.

Anna thought, "This cowgirl is indeed young, but she is old enough to understand it all."

Liza began to understand, and she sat down and became very quiet.

"If I stay here, I will have Libby for as long as I live. But I will not have my family with me if I stay here, and I will never see them again. If I go back, Libby will only live ... she will only live as long ... she will only ... ..." and her voice trailed off as her words began to get stuck in her throat. And then she could not speak any longer because she was choked up and filled with despair.

Anna looked at Liza tenderly.

She wasn't sure if Liza wanted to cry or just needed a hug. But Anna knew that Liza understood everything now.

Then after another moment or two, Anna got up from her chair, walked to the open window and stretched out her hand to pet Abby. They looked at one another. Abby gently pushed her head into Anna's hand to ask for a scratch.

Then the buckskin horse spoke.

"You know Anna," said Abby quietly and thoughtfully. "One time we were in a stall together at a competition back home. You were feeling very chatty and you were brushing me and taking care of me. I was standing there listening to you. And you said that you would take care of me forever. No matter what ever happened, I would be with you forever and ever and you would take care of me throughout my entire life. Through old age and all. Any injuries I incurred or anything, you said you would always take care of me," Abby said.

Liza looked at Anna who was silently crying. The tears were spilling down her cheeks as she continued to look at Abby. There was a long pause and no one said a word. It was silent. Then Liza could hear birds outside and she could hear a gentle breeze and she smelt the fresh air. One of the horses stamped and shifted her weight but otherwise, everything was completely silent.

"And now, right here Anna, I can tell you the same thing. In this world, I will be with you forever. I will take care of you, Anna," Abby said.

Liza was silent. She knew she had just heard something very tender. Anna's tears were flowing solidly now yet her crying was silent. Liza noticed that Anna never stopped looking at her beloved buckskin horse.

Liza looked over at Libby and also got up from her chair and walked to the window next to Anna and cupped Libby's chin in her hand. Then Liza stroked her nose and rubbed her cheek.

Libby nuzzled Liza through the open window.

Then Libby dipped her head at an angle and leaned over and rubbed on Abby.

"You're a good mare, Abby. You are good for Anna," Libby said.

And Abby said to Libby, "I can see that you are good for Liza too."

Liza looked at Libby and Abby who were now nose to nose and standing quietly. It was at this moment, no matter what kind of adventures and experiences Liza was having, she knew she could not stay in this world with Libby. She knew she had to go back with her, back to their own world.

Anna had created something wonderful here but Liza knew that she could not be a part of it. Liza knew she had her own life to live, to create, to experience and for as long as it was possible, back in her own world, she would do it with Libby.

Liza shuddered at the thought that if she stayed with Anna, that Libby would almost live forever but that back home, she would only live the normal life expectancy of a horse. But that was the trade-off. Liza needed to go home. She needed to go back to the mountains and through the fog and do whatever she needed to do to go through and leave this world to get back to her parents.

And Liza knew that Libby would understand. "You only travel through as a pair," Liza had been told. So now Liza knew that was the rule about Travelers. And Libby knew that was the rule. As they looked at one another, Libby did not have to say a word. Liza knew that Libby knew what she was thinking.

Liza looked around at this wonderful home and the farm and she knew she had to remember every single experience she was having.

She focused hard on what she had already learned here and tried to anchor that in her head.

Libby nuzzled her once more.

Liza was proud to know Anna, her cowgirl mentor. And she knew she would carry Anna's strength and commitment with her forever, but she would do it back in her own world.

CHAPTER TWENTY-SIX

IT'S GOING TO BE FINE

Over the next few weeks, Liza spent a lot of time continuing to get to know the village and the region where Anna lived. It was comforting to know she had a safe home to return to after she and Libby would go off to explore. Some days she and Libby would travel long distances and just meander on different paths, always seeming to find different trails back to Anna's village.

Liza never seemed to tire of all the interesting architecture there in the valley and in the little hamlets dotting the lower and upper mountainsides. She enjoyed the different looks of all the chalets – short ones, tall ones, some with symmetrical rooflines and some with rooflines which slanted off long and low to one side. She especially liked the many different styles of mountain huts. Some were made entirely of wood with slate roof tops and some were made of stone at the bottom several feet or so, then made with wooden beams the rest of the way.

She got to know the different styles of making hay too. Mostly done with wooden or metal pitch forks, hay was manually tossed into piles up high in the air and later, often brought to storage chalets and tossed up into higher storage areas to protect from mice and other hungry creatures.

Those storage chalets were built on tall, stacked stone, stilt-like supports with funny stone discs at the top. This kept out critters and moisture alike.

As she and Libby would explore, Liza would sometimes sketch the different building styles she encountered. She made her sketches and notes in a special leather portfolio that Anna had given her. It was very high-quality leather with blank paper inside for drawing or note taking. On the outside, was a tin or some kind of delicate metal equestrian-themed design that was embedded into the leather with prongs. There were three horse heads in their bridles, with flowing manes. Anna said this was made for a special lady of importance, who had given it to Anna as a thank you many years ago.

Liza had tried to refuse this special gift but Anna insisted. At first, Liza wasn't sure if should could return to her world with extra items found in this world with Anna. She had come through to Anna's world with everything she had with her during her trail ride with her parents. Would everything she collected here be able to pass through and come back with her when she returned home? This leather portfolio from Anna was a new treasure for Liza, that much was certain. Especially now that it was full of her sketches from everything she was experiencing here with Anna. This portfolio was very special to Liza now.

Over all of this time, Anna was almost becoming like an older big sister to Liza. Next to her mother, Anna was one of the best cowgirl mentors ever. But having Anna becoming like a big sister to Liza, well, that was very special for her.

As an only child, although Liza enjoyed her parents and her special times with Libby, she sometimes had felt a little bit lonely for friends or for a brother or sister especially when the family traveled. Perhaps that was why she relied on her bond with Libby so much. Back in her world, she talked to Libby all the time, not knowing that Libby had actually understood her all that while! "Just imagine," Liza thought. "All that time Libby understood me!" Liza smiled just thinking about it.

The more she thought about it, Liza felt she was lucky to have so many strong women in her life. And here in this world, she had met several more. These strong women included Meia's mother, a few local shopkeepers who ran businesses by themselves and some of the other women in the village. These village women were kind to Liza and helped to teach her some regional German dialect whenever Liza helped with food purchases, buying supplies or doing errands or other shopping for Anna at their stores.

At Anna's farm, Liza helped with some of the chores and helped prepare meals as well. She wanted to do her share and to try to repay Anna's kindness as well as some expenses she was incurring as guests for so long.

"Liza, please don't worry so much. You and Libby are my guests! And you have already helped me quite a lot. Remember when you delivered medicines to the family across the valley when I was unable to travel to them?" Anna reminded Liza one time as they prepared the evening meal together.

One day, Anna was in the garden weeding. For some reason, she stood up and looked over at Abby. Liza and Libby were out exploring the valley and Anna had a little time to herself for her own gardening work, which for her was more fun than a chore.

As she stood up, she felt a breeze on her face and she was surprised. This one felt almost otherworldly, not like a normal breeze but like a voice that was whispering to her. She felt the breeze in her hair and against her face. Nothing was said but when she looked over at Abby, they both understood the meaning of what they had felt.

"It's time," the voice said. Anna heard it clearly.

Abby walked closer to Anna. Anna heard the rustling of Abby's legs against the grasses and she waited for her.

"I know what you are going to say, Anna," said Abby.

"You do?" she replied.

"It's time for her to return to her world. The timing is correct. She needs to take the map and return," said Abby.

"I know," said Anna sadly. "I can feel it. It is time for Liza to return. Her experiences here have been so wonderful for the two of us and for her and for her time with Libby, but you are right. She needs to return," sighed Anna.

"Wow, this is going to be hard," Anna said to herself.

Abby walked closer to Anna and stood at the garden fence. Anna leaned over to Abby and petted her nose. In spite of the breeze, Abby wasn't dancing and prancing. She was quiet.

"You are right, Anna. This will be hard for both of us. I have enjoyed my time with Libby too. She has become like a sister to me just like Liza has become like a much younger little sister to you," said Abby.

"You know, Abby, reading my thoughts is not such a bad thing," Anna said as she winked at her beloved horse.

Abby issued a soft nicker.

"It's going to be fine," said Anna to her beloved and trusted friend.

CHAPTER TWENTY-SEVEN

LIBBY FELT IT TOO

Liza and Libby had just come upon a beautiful little village church along the side of the road. It was white with brown trim, a steep roof and had a geometrically shaped spire on the rooftop. Small chalets dotted the hills.

"This is so beautiful," Liza said to Libby. "Oh wait, let me look around for any people first before you and I start to chatter away," laughed Liza.

Libby understood what that meant, and turned to look behind them without Liza asking her to do so.

First, they walked down the little road and Liza and Libby looked all around. The little stones in the country road made a crunching sound under Libby's shoes and Liza heard the light clinking noise of them against the bigger stones as well. Then they walked back, and they looked around again.

"All clear," said Libby. "You do know that I would sense if people were around, but it's always good to look," she added.

Liza dismounted and took the reins in her hand and began to walk back to the main door of the little church leading Libby behind her. It was pretty and peaceful here walking up to it and as she approached, she could feel the cool temperature of the walls of this hillside village church against her skin. "Who built this beautiful little church?" Liza wondered.

All of a sudden, Libby whinnied and shuddered.

"Liza, did you feel that?" Libby exclaimed, prancing slightly. Then she stomped one hoof into the ground, pawed deliberately and finally she stood patiently, waiting for Liza's answer.

"Uh, well, that depends," said Liza. "What did you feel?"

"That breeze. It's as though a warm voice was calling to me; calling to us. Did you feel it? Did you feel it too?" Libby asked.

Liza looked away and then looked up to the sun that was beaming down and she closed her eyes. "There it is," Liza thought to herself. "There it is," she said out loud.

"So, then you felt it too, right?" Libby asked.

Again, there was a pause and silence between them.

"And you know what it means, right?" Libby added.

Liza sighed. Her shoulders slumped a bit then she stood up straight and tall.

"I think it's time for us to return home, Libby," Liza said with a tinge of sorrow in her voice. She was feeling a little bit of excitement as she said this but also some tremendous sadness. This was all going to be a difficult goodbye. She just knew it.

It was still early morning, and Liza and Libby hadn't gone that far from Anna's farm. Looking down in the valley, from where the church was located, once Liza had mounted up on Libby's back again, Liza thought she could almost see Anna in her garden on the back side of her chalet. Liza saw that Abby was standing at the end of her pasture, close to the garden. She could see that it looked as though Anna and Abby were having a conversation with one another.

Suddenly, Anna and Abby looked up into the hillside, exactly where Liza was standing there with Libby. Anna waved!

"How did she do that?" Liza pondered.

Liza felt instantly curious. "Libby, how did she know we were exactly here, up at the church? Up at this church, right here? She and Abby looked up exactly where we were after their conversation ended and they looked right at us. Do you suppose they felt what we felt?" Liza asked.

Libby was thoughtful then turned her head to look over at Liza.

"If it's time, I think all Travelers know that it's time, Liza," said Libby. "I believe they are all connected."

The air was fresh and clear. The gentle breeze made Libby's mane waft around a bit. Libby moved her ears in different directions as if she was listening to something or feeling something or sensing something special. Liza always watched Libby's ears because they spoke volumes of information. Every smart cowgirl knew to watch the ears of her horse.

"I think we should return to Anna and Abby's farm, gather our things, and say our goodbyes," Libby said with poignant finality.

CHAPTER TWENTY-EIGHT

THE MAP

By the time the pair had returned to the chalet, Liza noticed that Anna had pulled Liza's bedroll and saddlebags from the storage room in the stable. From the looks of it, they were fully packed with each of the few possessions Liza had accumulated during her time in this world. On top of that, it looked as though Anna had outdone herself with provisions for Liza. It all looked heavy but would hang evenly for proper weight distribution on Libby's saddle. Liza was guessing that Anna had provided plenty of food and snacks and specialty foods for her journey back into the Alps to find the fog bank. She was sure there were special treats for Libby as well.

Liza dismounted and ran to Anna and hugged her.

"Did we feel the same thing, Anna?" Liza asked.

"Yes, my little cowgirl, we did. It's time. Now that you are a Traveler, you will always feel the same thing that other Travelers feel when an important moment is about to take place. It's why I knew where to look for you on the road by the little church when I looked up into the hills, and why I was able to see you right away," Anna continued.

While she was speaking, Anna had nimbly attached everything to Libby's saddle. "There's no turning back," Anna thought.

"I'm speechless," Liza said. "I don't know what to say. I don't know if I will ever see you again," Liza said. "I can't believe we have to leave. I know we must leave, but I just can't believe that it's time to go already." Libby was standing right beside her nuzzling her.

Suddenly, Liza had a fantastic idea!

"Come back with us, Anna," Liza said as the idea burst into her head. She knew she had to ask. The thought burned too brightly in her mind, and she just knew she had to ask!

"Anna, come back with us. We can be your family. My parents will love you too, I just know it," Liza cried out.

Libby nuzzled Liza even more lovingly, knowing her little cowgirl well enough by now that to hear that urgency in Liza's voice meant she might be overwhelmed with emotion and would need her even more at this moment. Libby was quiet but Liza could feel her warmth and felt her breathing as she stood very close to Liza.

Anna was looking at Liza with a calm look of compassion and yet before she even replied, Liza knew what she would say. Or did she?

"Liza, my little cowgirl sister, do you know the one thing I have never done in all my time here in this world?" Anna asked.

This is not what Liza thought she would say. She was kind of expecting Anna to say that she would stay and would not come back with them. But, honestly? Liza was stumped. She had no idea what Anna was going to say now for sure.

"I have come back in time. You and I both know this, and a few special people in my life here also know this. You have met a few of them including Meia's family and the Watchmaker. I have never really explained fully, and I think it's obvious, but I have never taken advantage of the fact that I have come back in time. I have used my knowledge to help others and my own ideas to invent some basic but important tools and instruments and equipment that save lives. I have used my hands and my mind and my experience to make a difference. My friend the Watchmaker and I are kindred spirits in this. He has never once asked me for any secrets for him to exploit the future. And I have never offered that and I have also never exploited the somewhat unfair advantage that I have," Anna said.

Liza was really puzzled now. This wasn't the answer to her question to return with her to her world again. Or was it the answer?

"But I have made some changes in this world with the things I have invented with the Watchmaker. And these are good things. They help people. For every tool that is a success, we also have many failures but he and I keep working at it. I make some money to sustain my lifestyle as an entrepreneur, as a medical professional and as a farmer, as I must. But what I have done while living here in this world has specifically made changes – even subtle ones - to everything that will be experienced later on," Anna continued.

Liza was beginning to understand.

"I think I know what you are going to say," said Liza.

"Yes?"

"It means you can't return. The changes you have implemented here have had and will continue to have an impact on the future, and your future specifically. It means you simply cannot ever return," said Liza.

"That is correct," said Anna.

"Being a Traveler was confusing," thought Liza. Libby rubbed her head on Liza's arm.

"Have I changed anything?" Liza asked, concern mounting in her voice.

"No, my sweet cowgirl, your changes have been tiny ripples which will not have a deep impact. You are safe to return," said Anna.

Anna thought for a moment and added, "But your experiences here have had a profound impact on you and on your relationship with Libby, you know."

Liza nodded.

Abby was standing beside Anna now.

"Let her go, Anna," Abby said.

As Abby spoke, Anna absentmindedly double checked the saddlebags with experienced precision, and then gave Libby's saddle a slight tug and a shake as a final check.

"Time to go, my young friend," Anna said.

"Oh, Anna," Liza cried, throwing her arms around Anna and hugging her tightly.

Anna thought she would die. Tears formed in her eyes. "She has to make her way back alone," the voice said. "Travelers must make their way alone." Anna felt it and also knew it was true.

She realized then and there that she was feeling the profound sense of pain that only comes when you have begun to care for and love someone in your life and you have to say a final goodbye.

She leaned over and accepted the hug from Liza, and then suppressing tears, wrapped her arms around Liza and squeezed tightly. "This is one brave little cowgirl," thought Anna. Abby bumped Anna and Anna smiled.

Liza adjusted Libby's cinch and quickly checked the tack herself out of habit, then stepped up into the stirrup and swung her leg over Libby's back.

"One more thing, Liza. Take this trail map of Arizona with you. I won't need it, but you will," said Anna. Liza scrunched her face.

"A trail map of Arizona?" she asked Anna.

"About midday, open it and you will understand," Anna said with a smile.

Libby hesitated for a moment. She knew what was coming next but she didn't want to seem impolite. She looked over at Abby and said, "Goodbye my friend. Take good care of Anna for the rest of your days," Libby said.

"Goodbye to you too, Libby," said Abby. "That's one amazing cowgirl you have there."

Liza got herself positioned comfortably in her saddle. She checked her saddle one more time, swishing side to side in it to make sure the cinch was all right. She took a deep breath and exhaled. She looked all around her. She looked around at the neat little farm and all that Anna had accomplished there. Liza looked down through the village and looked at all the buildings and the chalets and at the people going about their day. She nodded a knowing smile at all the experiences she had had and how much of an impact every interaction had meant to her.

As she looked back at Anna, she said, "Well, I'd certainly like to come back here, Anna. So, I guess all Libby and I are saying is, 'See you another time', then right? Perhaps I can bring my parents here to meet you and Meia and her family, and to meet the Watchmaker and everyone else? We can do that, right?"

Libby stiffened. Abby stiffened. And everyone looked at Anna.

Anna said nothing but the look on her face was one of intense sympathy and kindness and sadness and joy all rolled up into one. Suddenly Liza felt exquisite pain when she began to realize the answer to her own question.

She jumped off Libby and ran to Anna and hugged her one last time.

"I have to be a strong little cowgirl, don't I?" Liza asked.

"Yes, Liza."

Liza got back up into the saddle.

And turning ever so slowly, Liza and Libby set off on the road, tears pouring down Liza's cheeks.

CHAPTER TWENTY-NINE

MIDDAY

Liza didn't have the courage to think too much on what had just happened. One moment she was enjoying a trail ride with Libby exploring Anna's valley, and the next moment she felt a breeze with the voice inside of the breeze giving her a sense of wonderment. The next moment she was saying goodbye to Anna.

It was no use crying. She had to think and make smart decisions for their long journey back to the fog bank. That is, if she could even find it.

The past few hours, Libby had been chatting on and on about some of the experiences she had with Abby. Like the time the two of them had lifted the latch on the gate to the pasture and had gone wandering about the village while Liza and Anna had been eating their lunch.

It had been a sunny day and Libby and Abby were watching butterflies in the field flit from flower to flower. They had wanted to explore the valley on their own a little bit too. Libby was certain she had heard the butterfly whisper, "You can wander too, like me," and that is where Libby got the idea to lift the latch. Like two mischievous little ponies, she and Abby had gallivanted down the road by themselves, tossing their heads and being silly mares until they got distracted by an apple tree beside the road. Libby knew that eating too many apples wasn't good for her tummy so she and Abby paced themselves and then after a while, decided it might be a good idea to return back to Anna's farm. No one had noticed, which Abby and Libby thought was a good thing.

"I'm not even sure you are listening to me, Libby," Liza admonished ever so slightly.

"Apples, yes, I was listening, mostly," Libby said, shaking her head as though she was laughing.

Liza laughed.

It was good to be reminded to laugh and smile. Liza was determined to make this experience of leaving a happy one and not one full of sorrow.

Libby walked and trotted occasionally and finally, at about noontime, Liza walked them off the trail a bit and dismounted and took off Libby's bridle.

"I'm not sure which way to go, girl," Liza said. Libby's head was down in the grass munching away already and if she said anything, Liza could not understand because Libby's mouth was full.

"When we came to Anna's village, she was leading the way and like a big silly, I was not memorizing landmarks, did you?" Liza asked Libby.

Libby lifted her head.

"Nope," she said and she went back to munching grass.

Liza was walking about with her hands in the pockets of her jacket and was doing some heavy thinking as she looked at the trails in front of her. "Which way was it?" she asked out loud.

Suddenly, she felt a folded piece of paper in her pocket. She pulled it out. It was the trail map of Arizona that Anna had given to her. "What good is this?" Liza said. "It might help when we go back but it's probably pretty old or wrong or new or I don't know ..." Liza said.

Libby was still eating.

"Open it," Libby mumbled.

After grabbing a snack from her pack, Liza sat down in the grass. Anna had made some meat and cheese and butter sandwiches with fresh bread and had wrapped them in paper. Liza took one out and began to eat. Then she opened the map.

As she studied it, she thought she recognized something but then the shapes and lines on the map started to shift and move and shift and realign again right before her eyes.

"Whoa," Liza cried. "Libby come look at this," Liza cried.

Libby ambled over slowly, grasses sticking out of her mouth. This was Liza's favorite sight to see. Multiple times on this trip Libby had done this and it always made Liza laugh.

"You know I can't read," said Libby, "but I will look at the map with you anyway. May I chew in your ear? Is that okay?" Libby asked.

Liza laughed again, then looked down at the map.

In front of her, on this Arizona map, Liza saw that the lines had repositioned themselves. This wasn't Anna's map, it was Liza's. She had the map with her all the time and had forgotten about and laid it aside somewhere in Anna's chalet.

She had almost thrown it away. Anna must have found it and given it to her when they were saying goodbye.

But something mysterious had happened to her Arizona trail map. The map had realigned itself to reflect the trails in the mountains here, in the Alps! And more than that, the sign of the Traveler was marked in about fifteen different places within the map along their route. That must mean these were friendly and safe places for Liza and Libby to stay on the way home.

"These are markers for all of Anna's friends," Liza cried out. "Why, this map looks full of shortcuts through the mountains too," she said, dragging her finger along a particular route. "And these trails will lead us back to the fog bank, I just know it," said Liza. Turning to look at Libby she said, "This map is just full of Traveler signs! All we have to do is use this map, follow all the signs and we will make our way home!" cried Liza breathlessly.

"See?" said Libby.

CHAPTER THIRTY

THE PLAYFUL HEAD BUTT

"*Oomph*," said Liza. Libby had just made a playful head butt against Liza.

"*Oomph*," Liza said again, a little bit more forcefully, as she stood up, a perplexed look on her face.

Liza put her hands on her hips and looked at Libby. "Libby, why did you just bump into me?"

"I was trying to get your attention," said Libby.

"You don't have to bump into me anymore to get my attention you know. All you have to do is ask," said Liza. "You know, all we do is talk to each other now, so all you have to do is ask or just say something if you're trying to get my attention," said Liza playfully.

Each day, Liza and Libby had been climbing steadily and following the map of the trails that Anna had placed into Liza's pocket. They had seen the sign of the Traveler near several mountain huts and near some chalets. Sometimes they stopped and went over and said hello but often they kept to themselves and continued their journey through the Alps.

They crossed mountain streams as they climbed steadily higher and higher. They traveled up over steep mountains, then down into valleys, and past herders and milkmaids. They passed a mountain man who was walking a sturdy horse pulling a cart full of cheese and he cut a small piece off to give to Liza.

All the while, they kept their goal in sight. The goal was to return to the trail where they would find the fog bank in the mountain.

Liza was a little worried if this would work out all right but she kept up her courage. She and Libby never stopped their chatting and chatting about their experiences here in this world and even though both were excited about returning, sometimes they had some intense moments of silence between them.

They had stopped for a rest and after a bit, decided to camp. They had a routine now. Liza removed all of Libby's tack and prepared a meal for herself. Libby grazed and walked about keeping an eye out for danger. Tonight, they had both stayed up later than usual and had stayed by the little fire Liza had made.

And that is when Libby made the playful head butt.

"Okey-doke, girl. You have my attention. What's up?" Liza asked.

Libby got quiet for a moment and looked out into the distance. She was trying to come up with a good reply to Liza's comment about not having to bump her head into Liza's body or arm to get her attention.

Then she turned to look at Liza with such a look of love it was almost heartbreaking to witness. A stillness was in the air. Libby paused for one more moment and then she spoke.

"I won't always be able to use words with you, my dear sweet girl," Libby said gently.

"When we return, you will have to remember all the ways that I do communicate with you. The way that I speak to you. How I use my ears and how I close my eyes. You'll have to notice how I'm swishing my tail. You'll have to notice the kind way I look at you when I turn my head back to watch you as you're brushing me. You'll have to notice the way my skin quivers when you touch me sometimes. You'll have to listen to the sounds I make, the whinny, the snort, the louder noises. And if I'm injured, you'll have to look at the way I stand, whether I'm lifting a leg, or standing solidly or whether I pull back from you. You know all of these things already, Liza," Libby said even more gently, "and you will have to communicate with me and understand me in these ways when we return. I need to remind you of that," Libby said solemnly.

Liza had stopped what she was doing and looked into Libby's eyes. She dropped her hands to her side and stood in the most relaxed pose she had ever had in her young life.

The moon was bright, and it lit up the forest where they stood. They could each see one another's face in the moonlight.

It was very evident that Libby was standing calmly and so was Liza.

The evening noises of the night were actually very quiet at that moment. There was no rustling of leaves as though an animal was walking or scurrying. Even the branches in the trees were silent. There was no wind and no gentle breeze.

It was as though the whole world was listening, waiting for what was going to be said next.

For just a moment, a tear formed in Liza's eyes as she looked at Libby. Libby was looking at her very intently, very gently, and very calmly. They both just looked at one another for a while. And then Liza put her hand under Libby's mane and Libby lowered her head slightly and closed her eyes. Liza looked at Libby's long lashes, her nose and for a moment, she thought she saw a slight smile from Libby.

They just stood there together for a long time, Liza feeling the warmth of Libby, and Libby felt Liza's heartbeat and her love. And that is how they spoke to one another, as they knew their time in this world was ending.

CHAPTER THIRTY-ONE

ARE YOU READY NOW?

Over the next few days on the trails, Liza became quiet and reserved. Sometime later one day, when they were resting but not ready to bed down for the night, Liza did not seem as talkative as usual. It was a late afternoon on a day still full of sunshine. Libby was surprised that Liza was still so quiet.

Libby sensed that Liza was probably processing everything she had experienced and she knew that Liza was concerned about what it would all be like once they returned. Libby knew it was the correct decision to return and she felt that Liza knew it was good to go back as well, but every now and then Libby felt that Liza was hesitating.

As they had climbed higher and higher earlier that day, Libby had gotten the feeling they were getting closer to the point in the trail, high in the mountains, where they might find the spot where they could return home. The terrain was looking familiar to Libby and every now and then Libby would blow a hard blow through her nose after taking a deep breath. Libby sensed the change in the air. It smelled fresh and clean but it also felt like home. Liza felt the changes too but stayed silent. One time, after Libby had taken a deep inhale and exhale, she felt Liza tense up in the saddle. Libby was certain Liza also knew they were getting close.

On this day, with plenty of sunshine still left before turning in, Libby saw Liza pull out the special leatherbound portfolio that Anna had given her. Liza had already removed Libby's tack to give her a chance to relax and feel the last of the day's sun on her back.

Libby wandered over into Liza's direct line of sight and slowly dropped awkwardly down to the ground and perched there on her legs yet on her side as well. She looked funny perched like that and she knew it. Libby flipped her head and swished her tail.

"Ooooh! Ooooh! Sketch me, sketch me, Liza, sketch me," she said. "We need a sketch of me with the Alps in the background," Libby said playfully.

That got Liza laughing. "Oh, you silly horse! There is nothing so graceful yet so awkward as a horse going down onto the ground. I laugh at you every time I see you do that, you know," said Liza.

"What?" said Libby, feigning shock. "What? You think I look silly? What about this!"

Libby suddenly rolled over onto her back and began to roll back and forth with curled legs flopping this way and that, making funny grunting noises. Liza was sketching furiously to capture the moment, then, dropping her portfolio, she ran over to Libby and began to rub her belly.

"There are some parts of your belly that are super soft and I love to rub your belly, you know," said Liza.

"Trust me, I can't ever scratch there so yes please, rub rub rub!" Libby said. As Liza rubbed her, Libby began to relax and began to lie down onto her side, legs straight out, head out to the side, lying in the meadow grasses. "This is wonderful," Libby thought.

Liza went back and picked up her treasured portfolio and sat down beside Libby. She began to sketch her mare, lying gracefully and peacefully in the mountain grasses. As she did, ever so slowly, Libby stretched out her neck and body and inched her head closer and closer to Liza. Liza kept sketching. Libby's nose was near Liza's right thigh now and she could hear the scritch scratch of the pencil across the paper as Liza sketched. Then Libby lifted her head again, and ever so carefully, gently placed her nose and cheek into Liza's lap. She exhaled. And Libby closed her eyes.

When Libby had moved to place her head in Liza's lap, Liza had instinctively lifted the sketchpad up and out of the way. With her mare's head in her lap, Liza felt the warmth of her mare's cheek lying on her and could feel the radiating heat of Libby's body as well.

Liza looked off into the distance and saw the flowers, the trees, the large stones, the meadow grasses, and further away, the steep jagged mountains that were so beautiful to behold.

Liza's right hand went to Libby's face and she began to pet and rub on Libby's face and cheek. Libby closed her eyes as Liza rubbed further down along her neck and straightened out Libby's mane.

Libby opened one eye and saw that Liza was crying.

"Why does this all have to end, Libby? Why?"

Libby nestled more deeply into Liza's lap and breathed in and out. Liza looked down and saw the nostrils flaring gently as Libby breathed. Libby's lower lip was relaxed and drooping ever so slightly. Realizing how relaxed her mare was, and this trusting loving moment she was experiencing with Libby, she stayed quiet and did not ask 'why' anymore. She stroked Libby and felt her muscles and her warmth.

They stayed like that for a long time.

Suddenly, Liza tensed for a moment. "Oh no," she said. Just like that, she saw the fog bank immediately ahead on their trail. "Oh no," she said again.

Her next words, she practically yelled.

"*NO!*" said Liza. "I can't. I can't. You and I won't be the same. It's the end of everything. I want to go back but I can't. I just can't. It's the end," Liza cried out.

And then Libby heard Liza burst into tears. Deep sobbing tears of an unbearable level of sorrow that Libby had never ever heard from her young mistress. Libby knew that Liza was inconsolable. The crying was deep and painful and from the heart. Liza turned slightly away from Libby and there in the grass, wrapped her arms around her knees trying to console herself.

Libby got up. She shook herself and took a few steps forward and flattening her head and stretching out her neck long and straight, Libby shook her entire body once again. Libby looked to the right and saw the fog. She knew what it meant and her heart ached too.

Libby walked a few steps back to Liza and lowering her head, nuzzled Liza with such exquisite gentleness that Liza stopped crying. She lifted her head to look into Libby's eyes. Instinctively, Liza brought her hand up to Libby's forehead and began to caress it.

Libby looked back ahead to the fog bank on the trail. Then she looked back as Liza. "Stand up Liza and get my tack on me. Would you do that please?" Libby asked. Liza looked like she was snapping out of her moment of sorrow. And listening to Libby's instructions, she stood up, walked over to where she had placed the saddle and the other tack, and tacked up Libby like she had done hundreds of times before. "When you have finished, please stand in front of me Liza. I need to tell you something," Libby said.

Liza adjusted the breast collar, ran her hand down the saddle pad and adjusted it. Liza checked the cinch, and then she checked the back cinch. Liza checked the saddle bags, and then she put the bridle back on. She took her time. She stood up straight and adjusted her hat. Liza tucked her shirt in better, straightened her jeans and adjusted her coat tugging it down in the front and in the back. She wiped the grasses and dust and dirt off her butt and her knees. She lifted up one foot and placing the toe behind her opposite calf, did a quick polish of her boot against her jeans. Then she did her other boot in the same manner.

She pushed some hair behind her ears and she wiped the tears from her face. Then she walked to the front of Libby and stood there.

"I'm frightened, Libby," she said.

"Don't be," said Libby.

There was a long pause. Liza tried to collect herself as she listened to the sounds there in the mountains. A marmot whistled somewhere higher up on the mountain, and Liza heard the pine trees rustle and sway.

"Liza, my dearest cowgirl, it's not the end, my dear. Oh, certainly not. My little cowgirl friend, this is just the beginning."

Liza's eyes shot open wide and her face brightened and she smiled and she became that determined little cowgirl Libby knew and loved.

"Are you ready, now?" Libby asked.

Liza flung her arms around Libby's neck and hugged her. And then wordlessly, Liza ran to Libby's side and holding the reins, jumped up into the saddle. Beams of sunlight shined down on Liza's blond ponytail as she flicked it back into place.

And then, gloriously and powerfully, and with mane and tail flying, Libby ran into the fog bank.

CHAPTER THIRTY-TWO

WHAT BELLE KNEW

"Mama! Papa! I'm back! We're back! Libby and I are back! We were gone for a long time but we're back," Liza cried.

Just down the hillside on the trail, Liza could see her parents. They were looking intently at the ground. Her father had dismounted and was scouring the trail. Her mother was on horseback and was looking left and right all over the trail.

Liza realized, from a distance, that her father had been looking for hoof prints. Her father was an expert tracker and would have known what Libby's shoe would have looked like in the dirt and sand.

Liza's heart ached for a moment knowing that her parents had tracked Libby's hoof prints up these trails and must have been scared when they saw the trail had vanished. She could not imagine what they had felt watching their trail disappear and not knowing what had happened all these weeks. But the day was as bright and sunny as the day she had first left. How long *had* she been gone?

"Papa, I'm back!" she cried again.

Both of her parents turned around. Her mother turned Belle with a click of her mouth and a nudge of her leg and trotted quickly and then went up into a lope as she and Belle came zipping up the trail to Liza.

Liza's mother and Belle came to a quick stop. Liza and Libby trotted up to Belle and Liza put her hand on her mother's knee and looked up at her. Then she reached out and hugged her mother tightly, nearly falling off Libby.

"Mama, I'm back! I was gone a long time and I met people from all over and I was in the mountains and I traveled and Libby and I had incredible adventures and I met some amazing people and I need to tell you about *EVERYTHING*," Liza said, the words tumbling out of her mouth. Her face was lit up and happy and bright and calm and excited all at once.

"Libby and I went into a fog bank as we were racing up this part of the trail here. I was pretending we were chasing bad guys and we were riding so fast we went into this fog bank and then *BOOM* we found ourselves in another world. We went back in time Mama and I know you won't believe me but we did," Liza exclaimed, her cheeks flushed.

Her mother looked at her with curiosity, and a smile formed on her face when she glanced down and saw Libby's longer hooves and scuffed shoes.

"And Libby could talk, Mama, really talk!" Liza cried.

By this time, her father had run up the trail, reins in hand, with Dude trotting along behind him. While Liza and her mother talked and laughed and hugged and cried with joy all at once, Belle looked at Libby, took a step closer and nuzzled her. Even though Dude was only a few steps away, he called out loudly to Libby, and Libby called right back. The little herd was excited.

Liza dismounted and ran into her father's arms. He had knelt down on one knee, relief on his face, and was hugging Liza as tightly as he could.

"We were so worried!" he said to Liza.

Liza's mother dismounted and walked calmly toward Liza. Liza let go of her father and skipped over to her mother and gave her a huge hug. "I'm sorry I rode on ahead, Mama."

She looked up at her mother and said, "I met the most incredible woman there, Mama. Her name was Anna and she was a real cowgirl too. And a doctor! She traveled with her horse too. Her horse is named Abby and she could talk too! And Abby and Libby would have long conversations while I learned about everything there in the village with Anna. But even though Anna had gone *there* from our world, she decided to stay. She had to help the village and she decided to STAY. She stayed there with Abby. So she will never be alone. Oh, Mama it was wonderful. And I had to help her a few times during our travels. And I learned so much and I met so many nice people. And Anna is the one who helped me get back to you," Liza exclaimed.

Liza's mother took a look into Liza's face, started to say something, but just held back tears and hugged Liza closely.

"I'm so proud of you," Liza's mother said. "And I'm glad you're home."

The horses were standing beside one another just down the trail and were nose to nose. They were content to be back together as their own herd of three.

Dude put his nose down to look curiously at a piece of stone there on the trail.

Belle looked at Libby for a moment.

And then Belle said to Libby, "I see you took good care of her there, didn't you?"

Libby turned to look at Belle and as she turned, she noticed the carved symbol of the sign hanging from the horn of Liza's mother's saddle. There it was; a little circular wooden disk with intricate carvings! Libby had never noticed it before, not really. And yet, it had always been there. The sign. It was hiding in plain sight.

Libby paused and stared. She stared at the sign for a long time. Then Libby turned to look at Liza's mother. Liza's mother caught Libby's eye and for the briefest moment, she nodded at Libby.

Libby stood absolutely still.

Then Libby turned to look at Belle.

And Libby said to Belle, "Thank you for telling me your stories all these years. And yes, I took very good care of her."

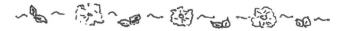

THE END

C

Reading the words 'THE END', as we all know,
is just really a moment to signal new beginnings.
And Libby will be with Liza on their new
adventures, every step of the way.

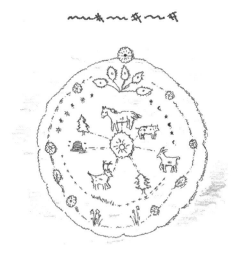

Thank you...

to B – For a "first look" impression of this delightful book, creative thoughts, edits and for enjoying the magic.

to N – For teaching me about fairies and dainty things.

to T – A fellow author who offered so much encouragement, and for the beautiful cover!

to C and B, S and T – For ideas of names for the other horses. Perfect!

to Dr. M and S – For taking care of Libby and loving her.

to J – For the joy of bling and pretty things.

to A – For teaching me about Arizona and to M for such wonderful care.

to C – Little girls deserve more books about horses! You are loved.

to my wonderful K – For everything. I love you. And Libby does too.

to my Father – For the painting of mountains and chalets.

and to my Mother – You taught me to pretend.